10-MINUTE IDEAS

FOR EARLY YEARS

Favourite stories

**Lesley Clark, Pauline Kenyon,
Jenny Morris**

■ **Quick activities for any time of the day**

■ **Links to Early Learn** **saving photocopiables**

Credits

Authors
Lesley Clark
Pauline Kenyon
Jenny Morris

Editor
Jane Bishop

Assistant Editors
Catherine Gilhooly
Aileen Lalor

Series Designer
Anna Oliwa

Designer
Geraldine Reidy

Cover Illustration
Craig Cameron/Art Collection

Illustrations
Louise Gardner

Text © 2005
© 2005 Scholastic Ltd

Designed using Adobe InDesign

Published by Scholastic Ltd
Villiers House
Clarendon Avenue
Leamington Spa
Warwickshire
CV32 5PR

www.scholastic.co.uk

Printed by Bell & Bain

1 2 3 4 5 6 7 8 9   5 6 7 8 9 0 1 2 3 4

British Library Cataloguing-in-Publication Data
A catalogue record for this book is available from the British Library.

ISBN 0-439-96507-1
ISBN 978-0439-965071

Contents

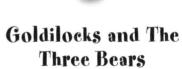

Contents

Rapunzel

Hansel and Gretel

Photocopiables

Introduction

Listening to and sharing stories is an important part of young children's learning which can deepen their understanding of the world in which they live. Traditional stories offer children the opportunity to actively participate in storytelling, to learn the structure of stories, and to experiment with words and repetitive patterns and rhymes.

Young children can develop their listening and speaking skills in response to familiar and traditional tales. The framework of a traditional tale provides a basis for adding detail, changing or adapting endings, and exploring moral messages.

Learning through stories

Traditional stories have stood the test of time and have been handed down from generation to generation. However, many young children now may not be as familiar with these tradional tales as their parents or grandparents were. Where children are familiar with traditional stories, it may be through video versions, which are sometimes viewed in isolation from the rest of the family. Nevertheless, most early years settings recognise the value of these stories, and carers enjoy reading them with younger children.

The six stories in this book challenge the children to explore a range of emotions, helping them to confront their own fears and providing opportunities to talk about different issues. They include fairy stories (Jack and the Beanstalk, Snow White), animal stories (The Little Red Hen, Goldilocks and The Three Bears) and traditional stories (Rapunzel, Hansel and Gretel). In turn, this collection of stories offers opportunities to explore a wide range of early years themes, bringing the traditional stories to today's children.

Planning for the Foundation Stage

This book provides activity ideas based on six different popular stories, with one chapter for each story. Within the chapter, there are ideas to cover all six Areas of Learning, as set out in the *Curriculum Guidance for the Foundation Stage* (QCA). For each activity, a Stepping Stone and an Early Learning Goal have been selected to enable practitioners to ensure they have comprehensive coverage of all areas. The Area of Learning is provided in an abbreviated form after each Early Learning Goal (see box right).

PSED – Personal, social and emotional development

CLL – Communication, language and literacy

MD – Mathematical development

KUW – Knowledge and understanding of the world

PD – Physical development

CD – Creative development

Using this book

The activities in the book are designed to be carried out in a relatively short space of time, with a minimum of preparation. Group sizes vary from two to ten, and activities can therefore be used to encourage teamwork and the development of social skills, or independent work and the development of imaginative play and problem solving.

Under 'What you need', a full list of all resources required is given, followed by step-by-step instructions in 'What to do'. Ideas to use with younger children and older children are provided for each activity under the heading 'Support and extension', and at the end of each activity there are a number of 'Further ideas', which give short suggestions for related ideas and activities.

Copies of the stories used in this book are reproduced on photocopiable pages 67–72. Pages 73–80 provide a range of photocopiable activity sheets linked with specific activity ideas to further extend the children's learning, providing a range of opportunities to develop skills.

Links with home

At the end of each activity, 'Home links' offers suggestions as to how parents and carers can help children transfer their developing skills into the home environment. The connection between home and school is a vital one and parents and carers need to be actively involved in ensuring the continuity of their child's education.

If possible, invite parents and carers in to see and hear the work that the children have completed on these traditional stories. Encourage the children to retell the stories at home with their parents, carers and siblings, and suggest that they tell them about the activities they have enjoyed.

Assessing the activities

Assessment is a natural part of early years teaching and learning and will be based on your observations of each child's success at given tasks or in specific situations. As each activity idea has a designated Stepping Stone and Early Learning Goal it will be clear what the expected outcome is and so possible to observe whether or not individual children have been successful.

Using the suggestions for supporting or extending children within each activity it should be clear when a child has achieved a Stepping Stone. A child who is managing an activity without the suggested support, or who is benefiting from the extension ideas, can be viewed as having achieved the appropriate Stepping Stone. Any child who still needs a certain amount of support to carry out the activity can be considered as not yet having mastered that Stepping Stone.

Jack and the Beanstalk

Use this simple traditional story to introduce some magical
activity ideas including a memory game, retelling the
story and making individual castle shape models
and a group wall display. These activities can
help extend children's vocabulary and
improve sequencing skills.

The giant's treasure

What you need
Selected personal items (see Preparation); card; felt-tipped pens.

Preparation
Ask the children and adult helpers to bring in things from home that are
precious to them such as photographs, souvenirs, clothes, objects, books or
toys. Make a large title, 'Things that are precious to us'. Cut and fold cards
ready for labelling each item.

What to do
Remind the children that in the story, Jack takes the cow to market and gets
the magic beans. This leads to his getting the giant's precious hen which lays
the golden eggs.

Explain to the children that everyone has some things that they think are
precious and that while sometimes these are valuable, sometimes they are
special for another reason. Show the children the range of things you have
in your own collection, including some ordinary, inexpensive things which
are precious to you. Explain why these items are special to you. Ask the other
adults in the group to do the same with their items.

Invite the children in turn to show their precious thing to the group. Ask
them: Who gave it to you? When did you get it? Is it old or new? Why is it
precious to you? Where do you keep it? How would you feel if you lost it? Write
a label for each item saying 'This is precious to…(name) because (reason)' and
make a display of the items in a safe place.

Discuss how we should look after other people's precious things properly.
Ask the children if Jack was right to steal the giant's precious things!

Support and extension
Help younger children to answer your questions by giving them possible
suggestions to choose from. Let older children make a book called 'Our
precious things' and ask them to draw pictures of their special belongings
with simple captions.

Further ideas
■ Read *Dogger* by Shirley Hughes (Red Fox).
■ Make a treasure chest from an old cardboard box and make necklaces and
bracelets from 'beads' made from scrunched up foil and sweet wrappers.

LEARNING OBJECTIVES
STEPPING STONE
Begin to accept the
needs of others, with
support.

EARLY LEARNING GOAL
Understand what is
right, what is wrong
and, why. (PSED)

GROUP SIZE
Five children.

HOME LINKS
Invite the children
to do a survey of
things that are
precious to parents,
grandparents and
carers and to report
back to the group
what they find.

Spot the difference

LEARNING OBJECTIVES
STEPPING STONE
Build up vocabulary that reflects the breadth of their experiences.

EARLY LEARNING GOAL
Extend their vocabulary, exploring the meanings and sounds of new words. (CLL)

GROUP SIZE
Up to six children.

What you need
Small tablecloth; shopping bag; scarf; large tray with: two large leaves, two gold-painted hard-boiled eggs, a large 'giant's' boot (adult walking boot), five beans, foil covered chocolate coins and a feather.

Preparation
Cover the tray containing the items with the tablecloth.

What to do
Ask the children to guess what is under the cloth. Accept all their guesses, however unusual they are, but ask them to consider if the thing they suggest would really fit on the tray. One by one, reveal the items and remind the children where each one featured in the story. Tell the children to try and remember all the items on the tray.

Next, cover the tray up again and explain that you are going to remove one item. Ask the children to close their eyes, and carefully slide one of the items into the shopping bag. Uncover the tray and ask if they can see what's missing. When they have made some guesses, show them which item you had removed. Encourage the children by taking a turn at guessing yourself and pretending you can't solve the problem. Say that you will need them to help and ask: Is it big or small? What colour is it? Who does it belong to?

Let the children take turns being blindfolded with a scarf while another child removes items from the tray to hide in the bag. Remove the blindfold and see if the child can identify what is missing. When they have guessed, let them check in the shopping bag. If possible give all the children a turn at guessing and choosing.

Support and extension
With younger children, start with only three items on the tray such as the feather, the boot and the eggs. Build up the number of items when you think the children are ready. For older children, write the names of the items on card and place the card labels by the items themselves. Play the game with the name labels rather than the items, starting with three, reading them together and building up the number used as the children become more proficient.

HOME LINKS
Invite parents and carers to play games such as 'I Spy' on journeys with their children to encourage observation skills.

Further ideas
■ Hide one of the objects in the room and ask the children to find it, playing 'hot' and 'cold', giving 'getting warmer' directions as the children search.
■ Place a tiny ribbon on some dolls or teddies for the children to spot.
■ Lay the table in the home corner and leave out one item. Can the children see what's missing?

What comes next?

What you need
Sheets of A4 card; the photocopiable sheet 'Tell the story' on page 73; two sheets of A2 sugar paper; string; Blu-Tack; adhesive; broad felt-tipped pen.

Preparation
Enlarge page 73 to A3 size, then cut out and mount the illustrations on to card. Fold the sheets of sugar paper in half and run string around the fold; tie it firmly keeping a hanging loop at the top.

What to do
Explain that you are going to make a group book to tell the story of Jack and the Beanstalk. Tell the children to listen very carefully while you tell the story, because they will need to remember the order in which things happened. As you tell the story, or read it aloud, ask the children: What happened before Jack did this? Why did this happen? What do you think will happen next?

Next, show the children the cards you have prepared. Explain that some of the pictures for the book are jumbled up and will need sorting out into the right order. Hold up the picture of Jack and his mother and tell them that this starts the story. Put it on the floor or Blu-Tack it to a wall or the board. In turn, hold up each card and ask the children to decide where it comes in the story, leaving spaces in which to fix the other cards. Encourage them to explain their reasons for the order of the pictures, using words such as 'before' and 'after'. As you hold up a card, say: Did this happen at the beginning of the story, in the middle or near the end? Check with the children if they think the cards are in the right order.

When the sequence is correct, glue the cards into the 'book', one per page. Hold the book up and ask the children what you should write as a caption under each picture.

Support and extension
With younger children break the story down into chapters and restrict the activity to only a few cards. Retell the story a little at a time. Ask a small group of older children to work together to sort the cards and then explain to you how the story develops. Let them glue the cards into the book and write their storyline ideas on paper before choosing which ones they will write into the book. See if they can put the same cards in a different order to tell a new story.

Further ideas
■ Paint illustrations for the book cover.
■ Use computers to write text for the book in different large fonts.
■ Learn the 'Fee-fi-fo-fum' chant and recite it walking like giants.

The giant's castle

What you need
Several sets of shaped building blocks, in a variety of sizes and colours.

What to do
Look around the room and identify things which have the same shape, such as square floor tiles, rectangular windows or circular plates. Talk about shapes that the children can see and invite them to tell you what they know about them; for example, a triangle has three sides.

Provide the sets of building blocks and look together at the various shapes asking the children to tell you the names of each type and to count up how many of each type they can see.

Remind the children that in the story there was a castle, and that castles are made up of lots of different shapes. Invite them to consider together what shapes might be used to make a castle.

Give each child their own set of building blocks and invite them each to use the blocks to make a castle shape. Encourage them to start with some large rectangles and to lay the shapes flat on a clear space on the floor as they work. Ensure that they work safely and do not try to make their castles too high.

As the children work, ask them to tell you the correct names of all the shapes, and to count how many of each shape they have. Ask: How many blue cuboids have you used? How many small cubes have you got? When their castles are finished, ask them to say how many of each shape they have used.

Invite the children to admire each other's creations and to identify the shapes their friends have used.

Support and extension
Younger children will need help planning their castles and would benefit from working alongside an older child or an adult helper. Ask older children to work in pairs to combine all their shapes and make a larger castle. See who can use the most shapes in their castles.

Further ideas
■ Use sticky coloured shapes to make pictures relating to the 'Jack and the Beanstalk' story.
■ Paint big shapes on the playground or hall floor and play 'Follow my leader' naming the shapes.
■ Play 'I Spy a square shape beginning with…'.

LEARNING OBJECTIVES
STEPPING STONE
Begin to talk about the shapes of everyday objects.
EARLY LEARNING GOAL
Use language such as 'circle' or 'bigger' to describe the shape and size of solids and flat shapes. (MD)

GROUP SIZE
Small groups or working individually.

HOME LINKS
Ask parents and carers to help their children to make a collection of objects of different shapes, cut out from catalogues and magazines.

The giant and Jack

What you need
Large sheets of sugar paper; pencils; paints; paper; brushes; scissors; glue; backing paper; large paper labels; felt-tipped pens; life-size and miniature plates, cutlery, mugs, shoes, hats and pillows.

Preparation
Fix several large sheets of sugar paper together and ask a tall adult wearing trousers to lie down and be drawn around, to form the rough shape of a giant. Draw around the outline and draw in giant-style clothes. Repeat, drawing around the smallest child and complete this figure of Jack. Cover the display area with backing paper.

What to do
Encourage the children to help you create a wall display. Ask them to draw around plates, cutlery, mugs, shoes, hats, pillows and other everyday objects. Then make a corresponding set drawing around doll-sized equivalents.

Fasten the giant to one side of the board, surrounded by all the giant-sized paraphernalia, and Jack to the other with all the doll-sized equipment. Put a selection of large and small sized objects in the middle and ask the children to identify who they belong to. Add some labels naming the owners of the different items.

Support and extension
Ask younger children to look at the two figures and say what they look like. Introduce words such as big, huge, enormous, little, tiny and small. With older children, point to the different-sized objects and ask the children to say to whom the objects belong and why. Introduce the idea of proportion – the giant's possessions are big in comparison to Jack's, but they are not 'giant'.

Further ideas
■ Read *The Gigantic Turnip* by Alexei Tolstoy (Barefoot Books).
■ Make hats, aprons, bibs or belts for dolls and teddies of different sizes. Use comparative language to describe them.

The magic beans

What you need
Jam jars (one for each child); packets of mung beans, alfalfa or other sprouting beans; squares of cotton (big enough to cover the jar top); elastic bands; jug of water; sticky labels; pencils.

Preparation
Prepare a clean jam jar, elastic band and cotton square for each child. Have a jug of water ready. Read the instructions on the seeds – most seeds will be ready for eating after about five days or so. You will need to time the 'planting' activity carefully to ensure the crop is ready on a convenient day.

What to do
Warn the children that not all seeds are safe to eat and supervise them closely at all times. Show the children the packets of seeds and explain that they are going to grow their own bean sprouts to eat. Read the instructions and ask: How long does it say these beans will take to grow? Are they all the same or different?

Ask each child to pour in enough seeds to cover the base of their jar and add sufficient water just to cover them. Encourage talking about the process of planting and watering: Are the beans floating? What will happen to the beans? Why do they need water?

Put the cotton square over the top and secure it with an elastic band. Write each child's name on a sticky label and fix it to their jar. Put the jar on the window ledge or similar position.

Each day, ask the children to look and smell carefully and to describe any changes in the beans. Also, tip the jars upside down each day to let the old water out through the cloth and add a little fresh water – just enough to cover the seedlings – and gently shake the bean sprouts. When they are about 3cm long and ready to eat, rinse them and use them in sandwiches or salads.

Support and extension
You will need to help younger children by pouring the water and fastening the bands. Have their names written on the labels. Ask older children to keep a growth diary each day by drawing a sketch of their beans and the changes they can see. You could help them write the date and a short sentence describing changes under each diary entry.

Further ideas
■ Let a few bean sprouts grow really long and then plant them into pots.
■ Cook a simple stir-fry of bean sprouts, add soy sauce and let the children taste some Chinese-style cookery.
■ Plant other vegetable seeds such as marrows, peas, beetroot.

The castle and the cottage

What you need
Photos or pictures of castles and houses (from magazines); collection of boxes of different sizes; cardboard tubes; card and paper (range of colours); scissors; sticky tape; PVA glue; thick paint in a range of colours; paint brushes; pencils; paper; aprons.

Preparation
Prepare illustrations or collect pictures of castles and small houses or cottages. Arrange the materials in piles ready for the children to sort through.

What to do
Remind the children that because they were poor, Jack and his mother lived in a tiny cottage, and that because he was so big and wealthy, the giant lived in a very large castle. Tell the children that they can choose to build either Jack's cottage or the giant's castle.

Show them the pictures which you have gathered and point out the different features. Ask them to use these pictures to give them ideas for their own constructions. Ask the children to choose which building they want to make and then ask them about the boxes and materials they will need to use. Draw attention to the differences in size and the suitability of the junk materials they choose. Ask: Will that be big enough for the giant's castle? How big will your model be? How big would Jack's cottage be then? Try to extend their vocabulary by asking: Do you think the castle will have towers? Will it have a drawbridge or a turret? Encourage them to think about their model. Ask: How will you get the windows open? Where is the giant's kitchen? How will you make Jack's garden? What colour is best for the roof? Why?

Let the children explore all the materials available and then build their models. Leave the models to dry if necessary and the children can then paint them.

Support and extension
Help younger children to choose their materials and to cut and fix the pieces together. Ask older children to look at the available materials and draw a simple plan of how their model will look. Suggest that they make some moving parts such as doors that will open, a drawbridge that lifts up and down, or a garden gate that will open and shut.

Further ideas
■ Ask the children to explain to each other where the different parts of the story happen in their models.
■ Go for a walk around the neighbourhood looking at different buildings and deciding what they are used for – shops, houses, offices, doctors' surgeries and so on.
■ Build different sized houses out of LEGO or construction kits.
■ Draw a simple map and ask children to tell a story about their journey, using the map to prompt them and including all of the places they pass.

Up we grow!

LEARNING OBJECTIVES

STEPPING STONE
Combine and repeat a range of movements.

EARLY LEARNING GOAL
Move with control and coordination. (PD)

GROUP SIZE
Whole class.

What you need
Cassette tapes of recorded music; glockenspiel or xylophone and beaters; large empty space.

Preparation
Either make tapes of the children's own growing and climbing/descending music (see 'Up and down the beanstalk' page 15) or use other suitable music such as *The Lark Ascending* by Vaughan Williams, or *Morning* by Grieg.

What to do
Tell the children they are going to make up a dance in which they will grow just like the magic beanstalk. Ask them to each find a space and to listen carefully to the music you are going to play. Talk about how seeds grow and ask the children how they could show this in their dance. Ask them to choose which part of their bodies will grow up first, last, the highest. Will they grow up straight or twirl round? Encourage them to develop their own ideas.

Play the instrument slowly, working from the lower to the higher notes. Ask the children to start by imagining that they are the magic beans asleep in their seed cases, and that they 'grow' very slowly in time with the music. Repeat the exercise several times, varying the speed of the music, and adding growing and shrinking. Invite the children to demonstrate their dances to the other children.

Next ask the children to listen to the cassette tapes and to make up their own growing dance in time with the music. Encourage the children to contribute their own suggestions and demonstrate their ideas.

Support and extension
Let younger children imagine their beanstalk can move around, twisting and turning as it goes, then sinking slowly down again. Allow older children to work in pairs to make up a growing dance together, or let some children play the music for the other children to dance to.

Further ideas
■ Move to music which sounds like Jack climbing the beanstalk, giants moving, magic hens and harps.
■ Learn some activity rhymes such as 'The Farmer's in his Den' or 'Here We Go Round the Mulberry Bush'.

HOME LINKS
Encourage parents and carers to support their children in enjoying physical activity by letting them join gym or dance groups, or by playing in the park with them.

Up and down the beanstalk

What you need
Range of untuned percussion instruments such as bells, tambourines, clappers/castanets, maracas, drums or home-made shakers and blocks; tuned percussion instruments such as chime bars, glockenspiel or xylophone and different beaters; cassette recorder.

What to do
Tell the children that they are going to compose some special music to sound like the magic beans growing and Jack and the giant on the beanstalk. Hold up each untuned percussion instrument in turn and show them how it can be played. Ask: How can we make gentle/loud music? Ask them to tell you how their instrument makes its sound and talk about the different types of sound they make.

Distribute the instruments and ask them each to play their instruments softly like the beans beginning to grow, getting louder as the beanstalk grows. Ask a volunteer to conduct the music from when it starts, as it gets louder and until it stops.

Then demonstrate the tuned instruments, showing how the notes can get higher or lower. Let the children take turns to play bean-growing music. Reinforce the activity by asking children to play Jack's climbing music, Jack's flight down and the Giant's fall. Let them practise and then tape their composition. Then play it back to them!

Support and extension
Concentrate on getting younger children to start and finish together, watching for the signal to play softly and loudly. Let older children work in pairs to compose their own growing or climbing music, performing it to the other children.

Further ideas
■ Play musical 'follow my leader' copying the loudness or softness of the leader.
■ Classify instruments according to whether they are blown, beaten, shaken, plucked or bowed.

LEARNING OBJECTIVES
STEPPING STONE
Explore the different sounds of instruments.

EARLY LEARNING GOAL
Recognise and explore how sounds can be changed, sing simple songs from memory, recognise repeated sounds and sound patterns and match movements to music. (CD)

GROUP SIZE
Small groups or whole class.

HOME LINKS
Tell parents and carers how to make musical instrument shakers with their children using washing-up liquid bottles and filling them with dried peas, seeds, sand, salt or small buttons.

Jack's journey

What you need

Collection of large flat leaves or large cut-out leaf shapes; thick mixed paint in several different shades of green; sheets of foam (larger than the leaves); plastic plates or containers; large brushes; large sheets of paper; scissors.

Preparation

Place the foam sheets on the plates or containers. Tip the paint on to the foam and work the colour well into it by twisting it or by using a large brush.

What to do

Tell the children that they are going to make a beanstalk out of leaf prints. Show them the different leaves and talk about the shapes, extending their vocabulary by identifying veins and stalks.

Demonstrate how to make a print by pressing each leaf into the foam and then transferring it to the paper, pressing it down firmly. Carefully remove the leaf to reveal the print. When they are ready to try, let each child print several different leaves in different shades of green and leave them to dry. Ask the children to look at the different shades of green and see if they can match the colours to the real leaves. Ask which colours are lighter and which are darker. Ask them to say what other things they can think of which are shades of green.

Later, cut the leaf prints out and stick them in pairs on to a display area to make the beanstalk.

Support and extension

Help younger children with the process of pressing into the foam and applying even pressure to the print. Use two very different shades of green to reinforce the difference, working up to more subtle differences. Invite older children to print their leaves in pairs ready for the display. Ask them to make other regular patterns with their leaf prints.

Further ideas

■ Count and number the leaves up to ten.
■ Print the leaf patterns onto plain fabric using fabric paints to make curtains for the play house, floor cushions or storage bags.
■ Paint a large block of each shade of green and make a collection of objects to match.

LEARNING OBJECTIVES
STEPPING STONE
Choose particular colours to use for a purpose.

EARLY LEARNING GOAL
Explore colour, texture, shape, form and space in two or three dimensions. (CD)

GROUP SIZE
Small groups.

HOME LINKS
Ask the children to collect large flat leaves with their parents and carers to bring in to the group.

Snow White

This exciting story offers opportunities to explore themes of contrasts such as different times, places, moods and characters, families, even sizes and kinds of apple! These activities can help children to extend language and mathematical experience and to explore issues in the world around us.

The magic mirror

What you need
Photocopies of mirror sheet for each child (see 'Preparation'); pencils; felt-tipped pens; crayons; scissors; adhesive; a collection of magazines; a large mirror.

Preparation
Draw a simple oval mirror shape onto an A4 piece of paper. Leave plenty of space inside the mirror for the children's drawings. Photocopy this for each child and one for your own use.

What to do
Show the children a real mirror and invite individual children to have a look in it and to say what they can see. Then angle the mirror slightly and ask them to describe what they can see in it now. Let several children have a turn.

Next, show the children the mirror shape on the photocopied page. Tell them that this is their magic mirror and they can choose to add their favourite things as a reflection. Draw in the shapes of your own favourite things on your own copy of the mirror to give the children some ideas. Talk about the things you have chosen and explain why you want them in your magic mirror.

Let the children look through the magazines to find suitable pictures to cut out and stick on their mirror shapes, or invite them to draw their own ideas directly on to the shape. Explain that because the mirror is magic, the children can choose anything at all to put in their reflection.

When the pictures are complete, write the relevant word under each choice. Ask each child to hold their mirror up and to say what they have chosen. Ask them why each thing is special.

Support and extension
Help younger children to choose and cut out their pictures, or let them draw just one or two special things. Let older children cut, stick and draw independently and ask them to copy and complete the sentence 'In my magic mirror I can see...' underneath.

Further ideas
■ Learn the wicked queen's chant 'Mirror, mirror on the wall' and act out being the wicked queen.
■ Ask the children to find out about other mirrors (such as wing mirrors, dental mirrors) and ask if they have seen fairground mirrors which distort images.

Family life

What you need
Magazines and catalogues; pencils; paper; scissors; adhesive; felt-tipped pens; sheets of card.

Preparation
Fold the card to make a zigzag book and add the title 'Living in a family' on one end.

What to do
Talk with the children about living in families, explaining that families can comprise many different groupings. Be sensitive to the range and variety of family groupings among the children. Talk about your own family, those who live at home and those who visit. Discuss things that people do in families and how different it would be living on your own. Ask the children: How many people live in your house? Who visits sometimes? What do you like doing as a family?

Ask the children to choose some favourite family scenes to draw or paint. Ask them to each supply a picture or a collage showing different scenes of family life and stick them all together in the group zigzag book. Write an explanatory sentence under each child's picture.

Encourage the children to talk about their pictures as they design them. Compare the sizes of families, counting how many brothers, sisters and pets.

Support and extension
Act as scribe for younger children helping them to write their sentences, and with cutting out small shapes. Let older children copy or write their own sentences and glue their own illustrations into the book, or they could make their own individual zigzag books.

- -

Further ideas
■ Make a pictogram of the number of people in everyone's family living at home. Include your own family in the pictogram.
■ Classify different animal families – birds, insects, reptiles, mammals or things that swim, fly, crawl or walk.

Who are the dwarfs?

What you need
Seven pieces of A3 card; scissors; felt-tipped pen; 21 pieces of card; string; fabric and paper in seven different colours; glue; spreaders; the photocopiable sheet 'Make a dwarf' on page 74.

Preparation
Enlarge the photocopiable sheet and make seven copies and cut and stick each dwarf onto a sheet of A3 card. Draw on seven different faces and characteristics. Sort the fabric and paper into seven colours and cut into pieces about 1cm square, then place in a container. Prepare glue and spreaders.

What to do
Tell the children that no one knows what the names of the seven dwarfs really were and that you are going to name them yourselves. Ask the children to suggest names, looking at the pictures for clues. Ask: Do you think he is happy or sad? Clever or silly? Sleepy or wide-awake? Is he thin or chubby? Neat or scruffy? Ask them to explain their answers to you and encourage them to suggest words to describe those features. Help by suggesting some names to them or reminding them of words in the story. Discuss the ideas, select seven and write these on card.

Now ask the children to look at the pictures of the dwarfs and to suggest some descriptive words for each dwarf. Select two suggestions for each and write these on some pieces of card too.

Finally, let the children work together to dress the dwarfs, sticking on squares of fabric in only one colour for each. When the decoration is complete, ask the children to find the correct name and descriptive words for each dwarf and to attach these to the pictures. Now suspend the dwarfs in a display.

Support and extension
Give younger children help with sticking and making the collage. Retell the story emphasising words which might help them choose characteristics later. Ask older children to make their collage to show the character of their dwarf, for example, untidy clothes, choosing a colour that suits their name – such as red for an angry dwarf.

Further ideas
■ Make up a group story about the dwarfs before Snow White came to stay.
■ Turn the home corner into the seven dwarfs' cottage.
■ Make simple puppets of the main characters in the story.

LEARNING OBJECTIVES
STEPPING STONE
Build up vocabulary that reflects the breadth of their experiences.

EARLY LEARNING GOAL
Extend their vocabulary, exploring the meanings and sounds of new words. (CLL)

GROUP SIZE
Small groups or whole class.

HOME LINKS
Encourage parents and carers to play word games such as Junior Scrabble with their children at home.

Seven dwarfs

LEARNING OBJECTIVES
STEPPING STONE
Match some shapes by recognising similarities and orientation.

EARLY LEARNING GOAL
Talk about, recognise and recreate simple patterns. (MD)

GROUP SIZE
Small groups.

What you need
The photocopiable sheet 'Find our clothes' on page 75; pencils; crayons or felt-tipped pens in seven different colours.

Preparation
Make copies of the photocopiable sheet to provide one for each child.

What to do
Hand out a copy of the photocopiable sheet and a pencil to each child. Show them that they have to match the clothes on the washing line to the correct dwarf by identifying the patterns. Ask the children to look very carefully at the different clothes and the patterns. Are they plain, spotted, striped, checked? How does the pattern go – across, downwards, diagonally? Is it dark or light? Point to each garment they choose and ask them to check that it matches. Ask them to look at the pattern on each dwarfs' trousers and then find his hat, socks and scarf to match.

Tell the children to join up the clothes to the correct dwarf using a pencil. They can then colour in each dwarf and his matching clothes so that all seven dwarfs are in a different colour. Ask them what colours they will choose; remind them that each dwarf must be different to the others and only have seven different colours available to avoid confusion.

Support and extension
With younger children enlarge the sheet to A3 size and cut out the items. Let the children sort them into groups, colour them and stick them on paper. Invite older children to count the number of hats, socks and scarves and let them complete the sentence that you write, 'There are … dwarfs and there are … hats and … scarves, but there are … socks!'.

HOME LINKS
Have a pattern day and invite parents and carers to let the children come dressed in stripes, spots or flowers. Have some spare items available in case any children are not dressed up on the day.

Further ideas
■ Match different coloured socks in pairs and count in twos.
■ Dress teddies or dolls in different clothes for different occasions.
■ Wash the dolls' clothes and hang them out to dry, counting all the garments.

When did it happen?

What you need
A collection of photographs or pictures of babies, toddlers, young and old people; A2 piece of paper; felt-tipped pens; Blu-Tack.

Preparation
Divide the sheet into three columns labelled 'A long time ago', 'Some time ago' and 'Not long ago'.

What to do
Tell the children that some things in the story of Snow White happened a long time ago, when Snow White was only just born, whereas other things in the story happen when she is much older. Retell the story, asking the children to say how old Snow White might have been when events happened, and pointing out how everyone changes as they grow older and time passes. Ask the children to say which events happened first, later on and last in the story. Ask: How old would Snow White have been when she was a baby? Sent out with the huntsman? Grew up in the dwarfs' cottage? Was tricked by the evil queen? Married the prince? Stress the passing of time and how some things happened a longer time ago than others.

Next, tell the children that you are going to sort some pictures of people you have collected according to how long ago they were born. Show the children the columns and read the titles. Then show the pictures one at a time and discuss which is the most likely column for each one to go in and place it correctly. Ask the children to look carefully at the pictures for clues. Is the person old, young, or in the middle? How can you tell? Ask them about their own families: who is the oldest/youngest? When the sorting is complete, focus on the similarities of people in the same columns.

Support and extension
With younger children, simply divide the sheet into 'Old' and 'Young'. For older children have a number line from 0–70, divided into tens, and help the children put the pictures on the timeline guessing approximately how old the people might be.

Further ideas
■ Sort pictures of old and new houses, everyday things, cars, toys and so on.
■ Make timeline of a week to show when different things happen such as television programmes or nursery/school events.
■ Start a weekly group diary.

Dwarfs at work

What you need
Some large boxes; paper plates; split pins; thick paints; brushes; string; card;
scissors.

Preparation
Make sure you have four plates for each box and a sufficient quantity of split
pins. Remove any sharp staples in the boxes.

What to do
Explain that you are going to make trucks for the seven dwarfs to put their
mined gold in. Point out that they will need wheels to make them move and a
handle or some means of pulling them along. Ask the children to talk through
their ideas before they begin. Encourage pairs to decide together what they
will do. Ask: Where do you want the wheels? How will the dwarfs pull it along?
What colours will it be? Why? Which dwarf will it belong to? Show the chidlren
all of the different materials you have available.

Let the children work in pairs to design their trucks, showing you where the
wheels and pulling device will go. When they have decided on how they will
make their truck, help the children fix the different parts in place, making holes
where needed for the string, and using split pins to connect sections. Let the
children finish the models by painting them carefully with thick paint to cover
up any wording on the boxes. When the models are complete encourage the
children to explain to each other how they made them.

Support and extension
Give help to younger children in positioning the wheels and handle. See if
older children can think of any different ways of making wheels which will go
round. Let them explore construction kits for ideas for their box model.

Further ideas
■ Learn to sing 'Heigh Ho, Heigh Ho, it's off to work we go!'.
■ Make gold nuggets from play dough, painted clay or Plasticine.
■ Invent a 'going to work, mining the gold and coming home' dance.
■ Make a large truck from a robust construction kit and test its strength with
a heavy load.

Different places

What you need
A collection of different sized and shaped boxes and containers; tubes, other reclaimed materials; card; adhesive; scissors; pebbles; sand; lolly sticks; used matchsticks; twigs; Plasticine; straw or raffia; thick paint; palettes; brushes; cardboard; pictures of castles, cottages, woods and mountains.

Preparation
Sort the materials into groups of things that would be useful to make a castle, a cottage, woods, and a goldmine entrance.

What to do
Tell the children that there are many different places in the Snow White story. Ask them to remember the evil queen's castle, the forest and the dwarfs' cottage. Talk about the differences in surroundings (such as the goldmine in the mountains). Tell them that they are going to make the different places so that you can compare them. Look at the pictures together and ask: What would a castle be like? Is it larger or smaller than a cottage? What would it be built of? What might a cottage be made of? Also ask: Who or what would live in a forest? Where does the gold come from? How do the dwarfs get into the mountain to dig?

Divide the children into groups or pairs and give them the materials for specific models, such as twigs and Plasticine to make the forest. Make the models and use them to talk about similarities and differences in locations. When the models are complete, ask: What is the same about a castle and a cottage? What is different? Are your surroundings the same in a forest as underground in a mountain?

Support and extension
Give younger children more information about castles, cottages and goldmines before they start modelling. Help older children to label their models, 'mine entrance', 'deepest forest', 'Queen's room' and so on.

■ ■

Further ideas
■ Look at large-scale local maps and identify houses, shops, the school and other features.
■ Look at photographs of contrasting places (deserts, islands, hot and cold landscapes) and talk about the differences.

Heigh ho!

What you need
Large space (indoors or out); cassette recorder; tape of musical extracts.

Preparation
Make a tape recording with short sections (one or two minutes each) of music made up of different moods with a mixture of slow, fast, sad, happy pieces.

What to do
Talk about the work the seven dwarfs had to do, for example, digging and scraping for gold in the mine, pulling heavy trucks along, sorting the gold, marching to and from work, doing the chores and gardening. Ask the children to demonstrate appropriate movements for each action. Let the children describe their actions. Ask: Which parts of your body are you using? Do you need to make big or little movements to show digging? How would you move if you were pulling a really heavy load? Rehearse them and improve them.

Play the music and ask the children which movements fit best to the different sections. Let them move to the music, practise their dances and perform them to each other. Let individuals or small groups perform and ask the others: What did they show us?

Support and extension
Let younger children work as individuals, or pairs, on only one or two different movements such as digging for gold and pulling the trucks. Ask older children to work in small groups and make up a sequence of movements, changing from one action to a very different one, to fit in with the changes in the music.

Further ideas
■ Play 'Follow my leader', copying the leader's changing movements.
■ Have team relay races. Pass a baton trying to move the fastest and then the slowest ways possible.
■ Act out a day in the life of the dwarfs.

Dwarf music

What you need
Range of percussion instruments such as drums, triangles, shakers, chime bars, tambourines and bells.

Preparation
Ensure there are at least 11 different instruments. Alternatively, provide a range of beaters so that available instruments can be played in different ways.

What to do
Explain that the children are going to compose a sound story which will tell the story of Snow White.

Demonstrate how to play each of the instruments, and let the children listen. Draw their attention to the differences in sound and differences which a hard or soft beater makes. Ask them to choose instruments to represent Snow White, the evil queen, the huntsman, the seven dwarfs and the prince. Ask the children why they have chosen their instrument. What kind of sound does it make? How many ways can you play it? Can you play it loudly/softly/slowly/quickly?

Retell the story, conducting to indicate to the musicians to play when their character is mentioned. Ask them to show the mood, for example, emphasise the angry evil queen, the sad dwarfs and the happy, charming prince.

Support and extension
Help younger children to choose their instruments, or use some simple home-made shakers or drums. Ask older children to work as a group to compose their own section of the story, such as the discovery of the dwarfs' house or the wedding scene.

Further ideas
■ Tape the composition and use it for dance or drama work.
■ Listen to music showing different moods (sad/joyful/soothing/discordant).
■ Invite the children to make up words for a Snow White song to a familiar tune such as 'London's Burning' or 'Ring-a-ring o' Roses'.

Suspended dwarf characters

LEARNING OBJECTIVES

STEPPING STONE
Work creatively on a large or small scale.

EARLY LEARNING GOAL
Explore colour, texture, shape, form and space in two or three dimensions. (CD)

GROUP SIZE
Small groups.

What you need
At least 14 sheets of A4 card or packing case cardboard; Sellotape; pencils; scissors; glue; spreaders; fabric scraps in seven different colours; wool scraps; string.

Preparation
Sort the fabric scraps into seven colours and cut them into small pieces. Tape the card together in pairs to make double length sheets.

What to do
Choose seven children and ask them to lie down on the card sheets. Carefully draw round their bodies to make dwarf shapes. Adjust them where necessary and add a hat. Draw in guidelines for the beard, trousers, belt, waistcoats and boots on both sides of the figures.

Let the children select one colour and stick on shades of that colour to dress their dwarf, adding beards, glasses and so on to complete the characters. Encourage the children to select their fabrics carefully by asking: What would look good as a belt? Why have you chosen that fabric for his boots? How many shades of blue can you count?

Let the children draw in the facial features. Next, cut the whole figures out neatly and complete the collage on the reverse side.

When the dwarfs are completed ask the children to talk about the size order and the differences and similarities in costume. For example, ask: Have they all got boots on? Who has the smallest hat? Then ask each group to choose a name for their dwarf and add a name card (from the offcuts). Finish your display by putting string through a sticky tape reinforced hole and suspending the dwarfs from the ceiling.

Support and extension
Help younger children to attach the fabric pieces. Invite older children to describe the different fabrics saying whether the texture is shiny, dull, rough or smooth.

HOME LINKS
Ask parents and carers if they can supply fabric offcuts for this activity.

Further ideas
■ Make other characters from the story in the same way.
■ Make smaller, individual figures that stand up with a card prop or support.
■ Ask the children to make puppets from paper bags, decorated with scraps and drawings and act out the story for the rest of the group.

The Little Red Hen

This tale is full of different animal characters and stars a hard-working mother hen and her chicks. It offers opportunities for the children to explore the rewards of hard work and to talk about working together as well as learning about the process of growing things and of making bread.

Many fingers make...

What you need
Timers; aprons; construction set; play dough; four pots of paints; four brushes; A1 sheet of scrap paper; sand tray; large wide container and four teaspoons; small-world farm set.

Preparation
Arrange the materials around the room so that groups of children can move between different tasks. Possible tasks could be: covering the paper with paint; building a farm and putting toy animals in each field; making a construction city; making a dough sausage as long as the table and so on.

What to do
Discuss times that the children work alone, and times they work together. Remind them that Hen didn't want to work alone, and yet only her baby chicks would help her. Explain that you are going to test out working alone and together, to find out about sharing and cooperating.

Show the children the timers and describe one of the tasks, such as covering the sheet of paper with paint so that there are no gaps. Ask for a Hen volunteer and watch him or her struggle with the task for one minute. Then call for volunteer animals to put on their aprons and join in. Let the other children notice how much more has been achieved, making sure you focus on doing things together rather than competitively.

Model each of the activities with a different set of children so they all practise doing and watching. Ask how each 'Hen' felt working alone and then as part of a team. Talk about being fair when clearing up and how much easier it is when everyone helps. How do you decide about taking turns? Who decides what to do and how can you settle arguments?

Support and extension
With younger children, talk about times when someone has helped them to do something that they found difficult to do on their own. Give older children more scope to make mistakes and to describe their feelings when encountering difficulties.

Further ideas
- Make a display, showing how 'many hands make light work'.
- Make 'Helping hands awards' for children who've been especially helpful.

Helping hands

LEARNING OBJECTIVES
STEPPING STONE
Show care and concern for others, for living things and the environment.

EARLY LEARNING GOAL
Consider the consequences of their words and actions for themselves and others. (PSED)

GROUP SIZE
Whole group.

What you need
Shades of red, orange, yellow and brown paints; pastel crayons; drawing materials; gloves; hand puppets; writing implements; small pieces of sugar paper; backing paper; white board and markers; Velcro; a table for display; 'feely' bag containing small objects – brush, duster, pencil, rolling pin, ball and so on; scissors; adhesive; pen; card.

Preparation
Put up backing paper which will contrast with red hand prints.

What you do
Encourage the children to retell the story, ordering each of Hen's tasks so they are able to recall what she did first, second and so on. Talk to the children about all the jobs that Hen had to do, and sequence them together by drawing objects on the board. Remind the children of the 'Red hen hands' (page 36) activity and ask about times when their hands have been useful.

Hold up your hands and ask the children to think about how essential they are for eating, cleaning, washing, dressing, drawing and so on. Think carefully about how we use our hands for different jobs and ask the children to mime doing 'helpful tasks'. Now ask the children to make bold red hand prints on the sugar paper, using the other paint colours to explore mixing different shades. While these are drying, help each child to record pictorially one example of how they are helpful. These shoud be small enough to be concealed under the hand prints.

Look at your pictorial list of Little Red Hen's jobs and ask pairs of children to draw an illustration for each one, using pastels. Mount these and arrange them randomly along the bottom of your display board. Make Velcro tags with numbers on, and write out a label inviting the children to stick on numbers to show the correct order.

Cut out and secure the hands to the board so that they can be lifted to reveal the children's examples of how they are helpful. Finally, use the table space for a display of objects related to hands, such as gloves, plus a feely bag containing items illustrating jobs that we do with our hands, such as a brush and a rolling pin.

Support and extension
Help younger children decide what to draw under their hand prints by giving them two options to choose from. Invite older children to use the numbers to sequence the story pictures correctly.

Further ideas
■ Explore other uses for hands, such as clapping, catching and measuring.
■ Ask the children to think about how we care for and clean our hands.

HOME LINKS
Ask parents and carers to select simple jobs that their children can help with at home, to give them the opportunity to contribute to the family.

Musical requests

What you need
Card; the photocopiable sheet 'Farmyard animals' on page 76; pens; simple pitched instrument such as a recorder.

Preparation
Copy the photocopiable page onto card and cut out the animal cards to match the farmyard creatures used in your story.

What to do
Explain to the children that they're going to help put Hen's questions and the animals' replies to music. Say the phrases together and notice how voices naturally go up and down as we speak. Use the recorder to demonstrate high and low notes and then make these contrasts with your voice.

Ask the first part of Hen's question, 'Who will help me…?' and point out that we can say words at different speeds too. Put your question to a simple tune as you tap out the beat with your fingers. Repeat in the same way with your animal replies, encouraging the children to join in with you.

Once the children are more confident, talk about the various animals' characteristics so that their 'reply' varies in pitch, tone and tempo. Use words such as beat, rhythm and speed to focus on tempo, encouraging strong contrasts. Ask: How would the cat sing? Would the pig sing in the same way? Show me how.

Deal out the animal cards to different children and ask the remaining children to take turns at being Hen, encouraging all of them to have a go.

Support and extension
Concentrate on good listening skills with younger children, encouraging them to appreciate the variety of sounds produced, rather than concentrating on accuracy. Allow older children to be creative and ask them to count and tap out beats and to describe the changes in pitch accurately.

Further ideas
■ Make recordings of your animal parade!
■ Move in response to your tunes and rhythm.
■ Use favourite songs and 'fit' the words to them.

LEARNING OBJECTIVES
STEPPING STONE
Describe main story settings, events and principal characters.

EARLY LEARNING GOAL
Enjoy listening to and using spoken and written language, and readily turn to it in their play and learning. (CLL)

GROUP SIZE
Any size

HOME LINKS
Suggest that parents and carers provide some simple percussion instruments for their children to experiment with at home.

Who will help me?

LEARNING OBJECTIVES

STEPPING STONE
Use vocabulary and forms of speech that are increasingly influenced by experience of books.

EARLY LEARNING GOAL
Extend their vocabulary, exploring the meaning and sounds of new words. (CLL)

GROUP SIZE
Any size, groups of up to four children when recording.

What you need
Cassette recorder; cleaning materials; washing-up brush; bowl; cloth; shoes; dirty socks; construction bricks and other 'activity' prompts; whiteboard; markers; copy of the story on photocopiable page 69.

What to do
Retell the early stages of the story, asking for some volunteer Hens and animal characters in the question and answer choruses. Ask the children to think of times when they need help and record ways they suggest of asking for help on the board. Talk about the correct way to ask for help. Contrast how it feels to ask or order a request. Focus on words we use to ask for help, listening to how tones and patterns change between a question and a response. Encourage role-play games using the props, such as the washing-up bowl.

Now consider aspects of a daily getting up routine when we might ask for help. Ask: How would you get help with making your breakfast? What would you say and who would you ask? Draw visual hints on the board to act as prompts and then encourage small groups of children to rehearse question and answer refrains, taking turns in each role. Then ask each group to make a recording, choosing a mixture of cooperative and unhelpful responses to a series of four or five questions. Play them back and discuss with the other children.

Talk about different responses to different types and tones of voice, and how we can 'answer' without speaking. Decide which are kind and unkind ways of responding.

Support and extension
With younger children use role-play to build confidence in speaking and responding in clear, deliberate sentences and offer close support when recording. As older children's confidence grows, encourage a wider use of language, more elaborate responses and greater characterisation. Encourage the social skills involved in successful shared recordings.

HOME LINKS
Tell parents and carers what you have been talking about and ask them to give their children practise in polite exchanges at home.

Further idea
■ Make individual or large zigzag books; create drawings with speech bubble requests and make lift-up flaps to show alternative replies.

Lazy pets, lively pets

What you need
Six clipboards; six small pictures of typical pet animals (or similar size); coloured pencils; pencils; large squared paper; columns of squared paper; scissors; adhesive sticks.

What to do
Talk about which animals in the story were lazy and ask whether anyone has a lazy pet or a lively pet at home. Show the children the six animal pictures and ask them to identify and describe them. Make sure the children understand what is meant by lazy and lively behaviour.

Give each child a clipboard, one of the animal pictures and two columns of graph paper. Agree together one colour for lazy and another for lively. Ask the children to conduct a survey by asking the children in their group: Do you think this animal is lazy or lively? Fill in one square in the correct colour and column to represent each answer. Each researcher will finish up with two coloured columns that can be easily compared.

Show children how to make a simple graph with their results. Place the labelled photos evenly along the horizontal axis. Mark off numbers along the vertical axis to match the square count on the coloured columns. Help the children trim and stick on the columns so that the results may be clearly read.

Show the children how to count the number of children interviewed ensuring that this tallies with the number of responses. Give the children practice in interpreting the graph by asking questions such as: How many children said (cats) are lazy? How many thought they were lively? How many altogether?

Support and extension
With younger children limit the number of people to be interviewed and use mathematical cubes of two different colours (from boxes on which you have drawn either a lively or a lazy face) instead of paper. Help older children to devise a simple recording process and make simple comparisons with the results. Focus on what makes the graph easy to 'read'.

Further ideas
■ Look at other simple recording methods, such as putting a cube in the appropriate hoop, then comparing the tallies.
■ Find out about animals who are particularly sleepy or active.

LEARNING OBJECTIVES
STEPPING STONE
Show an interest in number problems.

EARLY LEARNING GOAL
Use language such as 'more' or 'less' to compare two numbers. (MD)

GROUP SIZE
Up to six children.

HOME LINKS
Ask the children to think about what pets they have at home and make a pictogram of the results to find out which animal is most popular.

Need it to grow?

LEARNING OBJECTIVES
STEPPING STONE
Examine objects and living things to find out more about them.

EARLY LEARNING GOAL
Find out about, and identify, some features of living things, objects and events they observe. (KUW).

GROUP SIZE
Up to six children.

What you need
Fast-growing seeds such as mung beans; mustard and cress; small pots and compost (peat-free); clear containers; toy watering can; set of gardening tools; pieces of card; objects to sort, such as a doll, a stone, a feather, a plant and a worm; two sorting circles; paper; drawing materials.

Preparation
Write out labels on cards: 'Living/Not living' and 'Can grow/Can't grow', each with a picture clue.

What to do
Remind the children what Hen had to do to help the seeds grow. Talk about the things around us and discuss which things grow and are living. Ask the children how they know if something is alive.

Look carefully at the selection of objects and use the labels and sorting circles to divide them into living/non-living and then repeat by dividing them into can grow/can't grow. Encourage the children to consider factors such as does it move/breathe/change/grow? Let the children sort the items alone and explain their reasons for selection. Now look at the seeds carefully and discuss where and how they should be planted. Discuss the fact that they will need a certain amount of water and light, and then plant them carefully. Look at the seeds together and discuss why they haven't changed. Ask: What do they need to help them grow? Consider factors such as light, water and soil. Ask: What happens to plants without any light? What happens if they have too much or too little water? Can plants grow without any soil? (Some will root well in water alone.) Make a weekly check on your crop.

Support and extension
With younger children make clear contrasts between living and non-living things and show them some simple ways of caring for plants. With older children think in more detail about the characteristics of living and non-living and of growing and non-growing. Investigate whether a plant needs soil and/or light to grow and how much water it needs.

Further ideas
■ Design a seed packet cover, drawing ways that the seeds should be planted and cared for.
■ Grow beans in glass or clear plastic containers so that their root system can be easily seen.
■ Make a contrasting collage to show what plants need to grow successfully and what people need in order to grow.

HOME LINKS
Suggest that parents and carers help their children to plant some seeds at home and help to care for them, watering them and checking their growth regularly.

Harvesting history

What you need
Pictures and photographs of horse-drawn ploughs, oxen, sickles, tractors and combine harvesters; drawing materials; chalk; crayons; pastels; paper; samples of wheat and barley, plus other familiar crops; the photocopiable sheet 'Then and now' on page 77.

Preparation
Try to visit an arable farm and invite a retired farm-worker to describe how things have changed.

What to do
Look at the pictures of farming machinery and guess what they are used for. Remind the children that Hen cared for her seeds by hand alone and ask them why farmers don't do this now. Ask them to think about the three stages of growing crops and use the photocopiable sheet as a talking point.

Ask one group of children to draw how Hen would have carried out each task, another group to use the photocopiable sheet and books to draw how this might have been done long ago, and a third group to draw modern methods. Help the children in their research, label each picture so that it can be used in a comparative display.

See if the children can recall how Hen planted the seeds and what she did to care for them. Ask them what we use to water plants and how can we tell when food is ready for picking (harvesting)?

Support and extension
Help younger children to appreciate how machines help us, by comparing doing things using machines and by hand. Help the children to keep their drawings simple. Ask older children to look more closely at the materials and design of old machines and notice advances in technology and the types of skills required by a farmer.

Further ideas
■ Cut a small section of grass with scissors, compare this with the speed of mowing. Talk about different types of mowers.
■ Find out how harvest time is celebrated around the world, and about traditional activities in your own area.
■ Ask the children to sort the pictures on photocopiable sheet 'Then and now' on page 77 into 'now' and 'then' and to practise ordering them sequentially.

Busy hen or lazy lumps?

What you need
Tambourine; hoops; props such as a pillow, blanket, book, sunglasses, radio, a skipping-rope, trainers, racket, soft-ball, dancing shoes.

What to do
Ask the children to find a space, moving as slowly and heavily as possible. Once in their space they should go loose and floppy, before curling up on the floor. Now ask them to jiggle each body part awake, starting with rapid toe and finger movements. Tell them to stretch out and feel their bodies getting powerful and strong. To the beat of the tambourine, ask the children to dart quickly around the room like Hen. When you hit the tambourine hard, ask them to relax completely. Repeat the game, looking for children who are moving in interesting ways.

Now place the hoops around the room, placing an 'energetic' or 'relaxing' prop inside them. Discuss each of the props and ideas for movement that symbolise them. For example, dancing and twirling movements could represent the hoop containing dancing shoes. Ask the children to make fast, energetic movements or slow, lazy ones in response to the tambourine. On hearing a loud beat, the children make a small group around their nearest hoop and decide how to act out the activity together.

Ask the children if they know what skills and parts of their body they are using. Talk about regular hobbies and pastimes, deciding whether they are mainly exercise or relaxation, letting the children appreciate that both are valuable.

Support and extension
Help younger children to understand the different types of beat and how they should respond to them. They will need help to work cooperatively. Encourage older children to develop unusual ways of responding to the tambourine.

Further ideas
- Make masks for Hen and the other creatures.
- Produce a pictogram showing the children's favourite playtime activities.

Guess what I do?

What you need
Coloured paper or card; plain paper; drawing and writing materials; scissors; adhesive sticks.

Preparation
Cut card or paper so that each child can have a page in a large book. Trim plain paper, labelling and writing paper so that it fits neatly.

What to do
Discuss what activities the Hen performed in the story. Mime some of these actions for the children to guess, before encouraging volunteers to do the same. Try singing the Hen's actions (to the tune of 'Here we go round the Mulberry Bush'). For example, 'This is the way we knead the dough...'.

Now encourage the children to mime something they've been doing earlier in the day for others to guess. Suggest that the children make careful drawings to show their mime poses of the things they love doing. Collect ideas, but encourage individual responses so that each child makes a personal contribution with a written or dictated caption. Share and discuss together, then stick in each contribution to make an action-packed 'doing book'.

Focus the children's attention on the actions by asking what's she doing with her hands/feet/eyes/and so on? How can you tell he likes doing that? What do you think she is holding? Ask the children why their chosen activity is special.

Support and extension
Offer simple mimes for younger children to interpret and copy. Describe each activity sequence carefully and fully. For older children, encourage creative and individual responses allowing the children scope to practise their own miming and descriptive skills. Let the children plan and present their page as independently as possible.

Further ideas
■ Make a collection of activities the children do not like doing and write down why.
■ Show a visual sequence of actions with one stage missing and ask the children to spot what's wrong (such as forgetting to pour milk on your cereal).

LEARNING OBJECTIVES
STEPPING STONE
Begin to use representation as a means of communication.

EARLY LEARNING GOAL
Express and communicate their ideas, thoughts and feelings by using a widening range of materials, suitable tools, imaginative and role-play, movement, designing and making, and a variety of songs and musical instruments. (CD)

GROUP SIZE
Any size is suitable.

HOME LINKS
Ask parents and carers to help their children think of one thing that they like doing in their spare time and to help them make posters showing them doing this.

Red hen hands

LEARNING OBJECTIVES

STEPPING STONE
Explore what happens when they mix colours.

EARLY LEARNING GOAL
Explore colour, texture, shape, form and space in two or three dimensions. (CD)

GROUP SIZE
Up to six children.

What you need
Thick paints in shades of red, brown, orange and yellow; mixing palettes; brushes; paper; scissors; sticky paper; straw; sponge; blue and green paint; pieces of card; backing paper.

Preparation
Prepare the backing paper, a space for your prints to dry and for children to print onto the background. Cut pieces of paper into rough 'hand' sizes.

What to do
Explain that you're going to make a giant picture of Hen among her corn, and that her feathers will be made from hand prints. Ask the children about their favourite colours, and name those you are going to use. Can they show you the lightest and the darkest? Are any of the colours nearly the same? Look closely at what happens when two colours are mixed and describe the changes.

Ask the children to select two different colours and to make three hand prints, one with each separate colour and then one when they are mixed together.

Leave the prints to dry while the children clear up. Work on sponge-printing the sky and use an edge of some card to print green blades of grass. Arrange the straw in among the grass.

Return to the hand prints and help each child to cut round their prints, showing them how to turn the paper and to leave a gap around any narrow bits. Overlap the prints to create a giant fluffy hen and use sticky paper to add the features – beak, eye and claws.

Support and extension
Experiment with only three colours with younger children and supervise them closely whilst they do their cutting-out to avoid disappointment. With older children encourage experimentation and mixing. Aim for accurate prints and less supervised cutting, with the children choosing how to paint and print background scenery.

Further ideas
■ Ask the children to dictate what Hen is saying and add collage chicks and lazy animals.
■ Paint other pictures using only 'Hen' colours.
■ Use a relaxing colour such as blue, to focus on mixing different shades and using the results to create fantastic patterns.

HOME LINKS
Suggest that parents and carers provide paint in a range of colours at home for the children to experiment with mixing colours.

Goldilocks and The Three Bears

This tale has a delightful sense of adventure and naughtiness, and children can share the suspense and enjoy the musical quality of the refrains. It provides an opportunity to consider relationships and extend numerical skills.

Take care

What you need
Large sheets of paper; pens; pencils; pastels; scissors; adhesive sticks; examples of popular play equipment; whiteboard; markers.

What to do
Discuss how Goldilocks behaved in the story and what she might do if she came to visit us. Look at the examples of popular playthings and use Goldilocks to talk through regular problems with caring and sharing. Emphasise the co-operative behaviour you wish to promote through this activity.

On the whiteboard, illustrate and label other areas of the room where care is required such as the home corner. Collect practical ideas to encourage being fair and discuss how to care for certain items, such as by cleaning and putting them away carefully. Make a note of things which can be altered and ask the children to help you remember by making their own 'Caring and sharing' posters. This should be done in small groups so that the children focus on working cooperatively.

Ask the children to reflect upon times when they have not thought carefully about other people. Ask: How do you look after your favourite toys? How would you feel if someone treated them badly? How can we remind others about sharing and caring for our things? Talk about playthings in your group, checking that the children are aware of how to use and care for them.

Support and extension
With younger children concentrate on one activity or type of equipment, giving a step-by-step approach to playing and caring for them and reinforce safety and social rules. Help older children decide which play areas to consider, showing them cooperative means of working. Encourage them to write helpful hints to put around the room.

Further ideas
■ Make a list of ways to 'care and share' in the home corner.
■ Make up 'I care for …' badges and posters to demonstrate how respect helps us get along together.
■ Produce weekly tidying certificates for helpful children.
■ Each week, give a different group of children responsibility for tidying up after activities.

LEARNING OBJECTIVES
STEPPING STONE
Begin to accept the needs of others, with support.

EARLY LEARNING GOAL
Understand what is right, what is wrong, and why. (PSED)

GROUP SIZE
Any size.

HOME LINKS
Ask parents and carers to encourage their children to help tidy up at home, caring for their toys and looking after them appropriately.

Guess it Goldilocks!

STEPPING STONE
Describe main story
settings, events and
principal characters.

**EARLY LEARNING
GOAL**
Sustain attentive
listening, responding
to what they have
heard by relevant
comments, questions
or actions. (CLL)

GROUP SIZE
Whole group, then
groups of six.

HOME LINKS
Provide copies of the
photocopiable sheet
for the children to
take home, colour,
cut out and play
matching and sorting
games with.

What you need
The photocopiable sheet 'Size it up!' on page 78; card;
coloured pencils; laminator (optional).

Preparation
Copy the photocopiable page onto card and ask some
children to help colour the pictures very carefully,
laminate if possible and cut out the cards. Play
matching and sorting games with the cards so
the children are familiar with them.

What to do
Tell the story, emphasising the parts that
are featured on the cards. Explain to the
children that they are going to play a
game where they have to listen carefully
to clues, describing an object without
saying what it is. Model this several times
yourself, by showing one of the picture
clues and then making up a short phrase
to describe it. Start by helping the children to
describe the object's size and shape. Think about
where it is usually found and what it is made of. Ask:
What do we use this for? For example, say 'I'm big and soft. You usually find
me upstairs in your house, and you lie in me to go to sleep'.

Encourage the children to volunteer to have a turn before breaking into
smaller groups to play the game. Shuffle the cards and deal one to each
player. Take turns to describe items and the one who guesses first keeps the
card. The game continues with each player taking a card from the top of the
remaining pile, until all of them have been described.

Use the game to focus on listening skills: How do you show someone you
are ready? and on social skills: How shall we take turns and decide who can
guess the answer? Vary the activity to suit the needs of your group, always
setting clear group rules for fairness and turn-taking.

Support and extension
With younger children use toy models so that the children can feel what they
are describing and they can focus more easily on its colour and shape. Keep
the clues in a large sack to play the guessing game. With older children extend
the range and quality of descriptive terms used, and find alternatives to the
comparisons of size made in the story.

Further ideas
■ Make two sets of the cards and use them to play matching pairs or snap.
■ Bring in a mystery object once a week. Describe it, allowing the children to
make guesses. If they can't guess, allow them to feel it.

Golden rules for Goldilocks

What you need

Examples of environmental signs and messages; shopping bags; whiteboard; red, green and black markers; pieces of card; colouring materials (limited to bold 'message' colours).

Preparation

Cut the card into sign shapes so that each child has at least one. Produce three simple, large signs with picture symbols such as children or a train, or words such as 'stop'. Plan your 'signs' walk.

What to do

Ask the children to recall what Goldilocks did in the story. Explore whether she was right or wrong, and what rules she was breaking. Explain that many rules are drawn as signs, and that you are going on a hunt for some. Look around your setting for signs such as parking, entrance, toilet, fire exit and warning notices and so on.

On your return, discuss the meaning of the three signs you have drawn, emphasising how important clear picture clues are. Ask why theses signs are short, such as 'Private!', 'Stop!' and 'No Entry!', or why pictures are often used. Ask: What signs can you read? Where do you see that sign and what is it for? Extend the discussion to symbols for services such as trains and telephones, and for shops and roads.

Refer back to 'Goldilocks' to decide what sort of sign the bears could have on their front door. Help the children draw or write their own messages.

Support and extension

For younger children give clear examples and draw useful picture clues such as Goldilocks 'crossed out' or an angry bear face. Help them to write messages. Encourage free writing and copying as older children expand their knowledge of environmental symbols and words. Encourage them to work with a partner to test whether their signs are understood.

Further ideas

■ Make a collection of local signs and symbols using photographs and large drawings. Ask the children to guess the location and purpose of each.
■ Draw and write symbols and rules for your home corner area.
■ Make up a short list of group rules.

Three in the family

**LEARNING
OBJECTIVES
STEPPING STONE**
Compare two groups
of objects, saying
when they have the
same number.

**EARLY LEARNING
GOAL**
Use language such
as 'more' or 'less'
to compare two
numbers. (MD)

GROUP SIZE
A group of three or
six children.

What you need
Three teddy bears; three sets of toy bowls, spoons (include one extra spoon),
cups, bibs; paper; felt-tipped pens; thick finger paint; shaving foam; materials
of different colours and textures; table; three chairs.

Preparation
Make three large 3s, using differently textured and coloured materials. Form a
large 3 in paint and take a print.

What to do
Ask the children how many bears were
in the story. Show them the teddies
and ask if there are enough. Ask the
children to count and establish the
number sequence to three, finding out
what is one more than/less than three.
Count and name each bear before
asking the children to count out one
of each of the toy objects. Keep one of
the small chairs back so that children
establish that two is not enough, and
that one more is needed. Now select
three 'bear' volunteers and ask other
children to lay a place setting for each.
Establish that you have four spoons,
one more than three and that this can
be used to stir the porridge.

   Show the children how to write a '3' and let them trace over your large
textured samples, describing the movements they make. Explore with the
foam and paint before taking prints of their own '3' formation. While their
print is drying, use sorting equipment to make sets of three, and write labels
underneath. Finally, encourage the children to draw three bears with three
objects and to write the symbols '3' as a decorative border.

Support and extension
With younger children, reduce the number of examples and equipment. Ask
older children to compare sets of different quantities below five, to establish
number value and to increase confidence. Explore different ways of recording
'sets of three' and write 3 in many different media.

HOME LINKS
Ask the children to
find something at
home (such as a
birthday badge) with
the numeral 3 on
and to bring it in for
a group table display.

Further ideas
■ Produce a frieze showing groups of three from stories, such as three pigs,
three goats and so on.
■ Compare the children's ages to find out who is three and who is older/
younger than three.
■ Make a giant 3 for a door display, sticking on sets of three objects.

A chair for Baby bear

What you need
Soft toy bear; reclaimed materials such as cereal packets, tubes, cardboard boxes; pile of plastic tubs and containers; cotton wool; scraps of material; scissors; string; glue; Sellotape; drawing and colouring materials; pictures of chairs from magazines; play dough.

What to do
Remind the children that Baby bear's chair was broken in the story and show them your small bear. Look at the pictures, naming parts of a chair and contrasting different types of seats. Ask the children to describe their favourite chairs at home using the same terms, and note differences between chairs. What type of chair would Baby bear use at the table? How is this different to the one he would sit in to watch TV?

   Next, look at the materials together and talk about making a chair for Baby bear. Demonstrate ways of cutting and fixing a cardboard tube to a flat cardboard surface, and show the children how to join plastic containers. Allow the children to experiment but ask them to practice first, so they don't waste materials. Let them decorate the finished chairs with materials, paper, felt-tipped pens or paint. Finally, display and discuss each model and invite the bear to relax in each seat!

Support and extension
With younger children, model shapes of chairs using the play dough first. Encourage all the children to make similar designs so that you can demonstrate joining techniques. For older children, allow a wider range of materials and greater experimentation, linking back more closely to the purpose of their design and testing out different designs.

Further ideas
- Make model chairs or beds for the rest of the bear family.
- Collect brochures and toy furniture for a furniture shop display.
- Make bear-shaped biscuits to share at lunchtime.

LEARNING OBJECTIVES
STEPPING STONE
Construct with a purpose in mind, using a variety of resources.

EARLY LEARNING GOAL
Build and construct with a wide range of objects, selecting appropriate resources, and adapting their work where necessary. (KUW)

GROUP SIZE
Up to six children.

HOME LINKS
Ask the children to bring in photos of beds and chairs from home or to ask their parents and carers to help them to collect pictures from catalogues.

Breakfast build-ups

What you need
Pictures and photos of different breakfasts, including baby foods; sample packets of baby, child and adult cereals; bowls; spoons; baby bottle and muslin; bibs; serviettes; mats; long strip of card; pencils; paper; ruler; scissors; table; chairs; highchair (if possible); low wall space; backing paper.

Preparation
Make up the baby cereals and leave them to cool. Lay the table with three place settings, one for each age, with a sample of each breakfast available. Cover wall space with backing paper.

What to do
Look at the place settings and ask the children to guess who they are for. Sit at the baby cereal place, put on the bib and ask the children to guess your age! If anyone has baby siblings, ask them to describe what they eat and how they feed. Show the pictures and discuss why tiny babies drink milk rather than eat.

Use this as an opportunity to consider how the children have grown and changed. Ask: Can you feed yourself? Can you sit up on your own? Why do babies need a bib? Think carefully about how babies need to learn to do things such as to sit up. Ask: What have you learned to do recently?

Let the children each have a turn at sampling different place settings, taking care with hygiene rules. Help the children to draw a simple card timeline. Decorate and mark with key ages before sticking on a wall. Now cut out the pictures of breakfast food and stick on the wall at the correct place on the line. Add helpful labels and comments as dictated by the children, and encourage them to draw pictures of things they could do at each stage (guessing for the adult stage!) Use the timeline to highlight personal development, change and growth.

Support and extension
With younger children concentrate on baby/child comparisons and help the children to develop a sense of pride in their personal achievements and progress. With older children look in more detail at physical changes, and at what skills they have recently acquired or are learning now.

Further ideas
■ Place photographs of family members along your timeline.
■ Make a visual record of typical and healthy breakfasts for family members.

Big bear, little bear

What you need
Tape player; recorded tape.

Preparation
Record a tape to provide samples of strong, slow and heavy movement music (for example, *Pomp and Circumstance* by Elgar), contrasted with medium-paced music, such as 'Spring' from *The Four Seasons* by Vivaldi, and quick and light music like Rimsky-Korsakov's *Flight of the Bumble Bee*.

What to do
Ask the children to find a space and to pretend to be one of the three bears. Ask them to show you who they are without making a sound and without bumping into other bears.

Listen to the different pieces of music and agree which bear each excerpt represents. Play the music and ask the children to move like the appropriate bear. Choose some children to demonstrate their movements to others.

Now make up a 'story' with the movements: sleeping in caves, stretching and searching for food. Ask the children to make these movements in a Big or Little bear fashion. Can the others guess which bear they are? Then ask the children to find a new way of moving around using a different part of their body, but still choosing to make either little or big movements. Ask: How can you move easily and quickly, and which parts can you only move slightly? Describe the contrasts as the children experiment. Ask: What are you using to balance on the floor and how are you moving along? Show me a different way. Describe how we can use our limbs in strong, purposeful ways and soft, flexible and varied movements.

Finally, play the music again and let the children respond creatively. Warm down by imagining the bears are preparing for bed and relaxing each part of their body before crawling off to sleep.

Support and extension
Ask younger children to focus on the quality of big and little movements. Encourage older children to travel in contrasting ways, exploring different ways to balance and emphasising the quality of movements, both big and little.

Further ideas
- Use hoops and quoits to promote movement and balance.
- Perform a bear's dance, incorporating happy and angry movements.
- Make bear masks to aid bear dances.

LEARNING OBJECTIVES
STEPPING STONE
Initiate new combinations of movement and gesture in order to express and respond to feelings, ideas and experiences.

EARLY LEARNING GOAL
Move with confidence, imagination and in safety. (PD)

GROUP SIZE
Whole group.

HOME LINKS
Suggest that parents and carers could provide some music at home for their children to enjoy dancing along to.

Walking in the woods

What you need
Scraps of 'bear-coloured' material including fake fur, velvet, warm materials
and wool; bright thick yellow-gold wool; crêpe paper; tissue paper; large
buttons; beads; scissors; adhesive; backing paper; large sheet of grey paper;
paints; colouring materials; a display board.

Preparation
Cover the board with backing paper suitable for showing the bears out
walking in the woods. Cut out paper into three bear sizes and use some large
scraps of paper for trees, the upper part of Goldilocks and the cottage.

What to do
Talk to the children about what the bears did at the start of the story, and how
they would feel setting off for their walk. Use the paints, crêpe and tissue paper
to create a dense cover of trees and bushes in the background of your board.
Make the upper part of Goldilocks using paper and golden wool, so that she
can just be glimpsed dashing through the woods and add a section of the
bear's cottage if you have room. Ask: What shall we use to make Goldilocks'

hair? How can we show that
she is running?

Next, depending on the size
of your board, help the children
to create a small, medium and
large bear outline (or their
upper bodies). Use the collage
materials to match shades
and textures to create three
hairy bears. Use the buttons or
crumpled tissue paper for bear
features. Finally, create speech
bubbles for the bears, filling
them with suitable captions.
Write out a label inviting
children to describe where
Goldilocks is on the scene.

Support and extension
Help younger children to find the appropriate materials for the collage.
Encourage older children to talk about suitable colours and textures for the
collage, describing different shades.

Further ideas
■ Make smaller 'lift the flap' pictures for finding Goldilocks or one of the
objects described in the story.
■ Make a display of bear-like textures and contrast them with cold, thin and
hard materials.

Who's been...?

What you need
Thick paints in 'bear' colours; pencils; felt-tipped pens; paper; scissors; scrap paper; mirror; pictures of faces.

Preparation
Paint three identical bear faces, then paint another three, this time using a different shade of brown for one, making a cross face on another and giving a third an extra large nose. Cut enough paper for each child to make six bear faces, and have some spare paper in case of mistakes.

What to do
Show the children your three identical bear faces and ask the children to describe what they look like. Now remove one of the identical faces and replace it with one of the different faces. Ask the children to tell you which is the odd-one-out. Can they tell you why? Use mirrors and pictures to prompt discussion about facial features. Ask: How are eyes/mouths/noses different? What changes a face from looking happy to sad? Repeat this activity a few times until the children are confident at describing the different faces.

Hand out three pieces of paper to the children and ask them to draw three identical bear faces. What shapes and colours could we use for our bears? Encourage careful copying to produce faces which are nearly the same. When they have done this, hand out the other three pieces of paper to each child and ask them to draw three faces that are different in some way. Suggest that they concentrate on changing just one feature to make the bears' faces different, encouraging them to make the difference as slight as possible. Now ask the children to work with a partner to play games of odd-one-out and matching. Can they describe the different bears to each other accurately?

Support and extension
Let younger children use a template to draw their bear faces with and suggest that they make very obvious changes for their 'odd-one-out bear', such as a colour change. Ask older children to look more closely at features and make the differences less obvious. Encourage the children to check for accuracy and try sticking on features using different media.

Further ideas
■ Make a collage showing the bears in their cottage and include three mistakes to be found.
■ Use mirrors and pastels to create your own 'portrait gallery'.
■ Ask a child to describe someone – a famous person, teacher or another child, – for the rest of the children to identify.

Feel it, taste it

What you need
Six different boxes of cereals (be aware of any children with allergies); bowl and spoon for each child; milk; pencils; paper; scarves; washing-up materials; tea-towels.

What to do
Ask the children what they eat for breakfast and count how many like the same thing as the bears. Remind the children why Goldilocks didn't like the first two bowls she tried and discuss how we taste things. Explain that they are going to test some cereals without looking at them first. (Stress the importance of following strict hygiene rules). Blindfold each child with a scarf and give them a tiny amount of the same cereal to try. Ask them to feel it, smell it and then finally taste it, describing each experience, before trying to guess the name of the cereal. Make notes of what the children say. Encourage the children to use descriptive terms such as

sticky, lumpy and crunchy. Make comparisons between the cereals. Remove blindfolds so they can see if their guesses were right. Now repeat the exercise with a different cereal.

Use the comments that were made to play a guessing game with the other children. Finally, let them each choose a cereal to try, first dry, and then with milk, noting changes in appearance, texture and taste. Compare their findings and draw simple conclusions.

Involve the children in washing and drying the dishes.

Support and extension
With younger children reduce the range of cereals so that strong contrasts can be identified. Ask older children to consider which sense they are isolating at each stage and encourage full, accurate comments.

Further ideas
■ Ask the children to design a packet or a magazine advert for their favourite breakfast cereal.
■ Make a pictogram showing which cereal was the children's favourite.
■ Use small amounts of cereal to create textured collage pictures.

Rapunzel

This traditional story has all the ingredients of a fairy tale and includes a happy ending for Rapunzel and the Prince. The activity ideas in this chapter allow the children to explore themes such as practising singing, comparing hairstyles, building towers and tying rope ladders!

Our hairstyles

What you need
Display board; background paper; A4 card for each child; PVA glue and spreaders; scissors; pencils; crayons; felt-tipped pens; stapler; labelling card; marker pen; mirror on a stand; textured materials such as strong raffia, unravelled knitted wool and some new knitting wool, curly pasta, macaroni, vermicelli, wood curls, crêpe paper, paper for pleating and fringing, fluted pastry cases, corrugated cardboard, bubblewrap, sandpaper.

Preparation
Pleat one piece of paper and fringe another to use as examples. Unravel some knitted wool. Lay out all the materials. Line the display board with paper and write a label with each child's name on it.

What to do
Talk about how people have different hair colour and texture. Can the children name hair colours (blonde, red, black, brown, grey, white) and hair textures (straight, wavy, curly, wiry, permed)? What does 'bald' mean?

Explain to the children that you are going to look at their hairstyles and then make a display. Remain sensitive to individual children's appearances. Ask the children to sit in front of the mirror one at a time, to look at their hair.

Give them each a piece of card and tell them to make a big drawing of their face and them choose one of the materials that is most like their hair texture (it doesn't matter if this isn't accurate!). If they choose the pleated or fringed paper, encourage them to make their own following the model. They can then stick the 'hair' in place on their drawing.

Staple all their pictures onto the display area and label it 'Our hairstyles'. At this stage do not label each picture.

Support and extension
Help younger children to identify their hair colour and type by offering two distinct choices for each attribute. Older children can aim for as realistic a match to their own hair type as possible.

Further ideas
■ Ask the group to guess whose picture is whose from the hairstyles. Then staple each child's name to his or her picture.
■ Let the children measure the length of the longest part of their friend's hair. Write the measurement up on their name label.

LEARNING OBJECTIVES
STEPPING STONE
Have a sense of belonging.

EARLY LEARNING GOAL
Have a developing awarenees of their own needs, views and feelings and be sensitive to the needs, views and feelings of others. (PSED)

GROUP SIZE
Four children at a time.

HOME LINKS
Talk about how hair colour and type can be inherited from parents and ask the children to think about their family's hair. Remain sensitive to any children who may not live with their natural parents.

Let's play hairdressers

What you need

Two or three combs; jug of water with diluted disinfectant; a packet of hair-clips; dustpan and brush; shallow washing-up bowl; clean old bath towel; two worn clean men's shirts on coat-hangers; scissors; empty shampoo and conditioner bottles; two cardboard tubes from kitchen towels; two mirrors (preferably on stands); chairs; tables; play money in a till; a toy telephone; notebook; pencil.

Preparation

Cut off the shirt collars and sleeves to make overalls. Cut the towel up to make small towels. Bend and crease the cardboard tubes in half to use as hairdryers. Make certain there are no real scissors available.

What to do

Talk about Rapunzel's beautiful long hair and invite the children to say what we need to do to our hair to keep it in good condition. Ask the children to tell you about any visits to the hairdresser's they have made.

Help the children set up a role-play hairdressing salon. Make a reception area by hanging up the overalls, placing the till, telephone, notebook and pencil for booking appointments on a table with a chair behind. For the hair-washing area put the bowl on a table with a chair in front of it. Arrange a pile of folded towels and the shampoo and conditioner bottles. In the styling area put mirrors on two tables with chairs facing them and the dustpan and brush underneath. Lay out the hair-clips and hairdryers and put combs in the diluted disinfectant.

Let the children take it in turns to be hairdressers and customers. Show them how to move their fingers in a scissor-like action for pretend hair cutting. Ensure that they put the combs into the diluted disinfectant before using them on each other's hair.

Support and extension

Let younger children be in charge of jobs such as folding the towels and keeping them in a tidy pile. Ask older children to write down the customer's names in the appointments diary.

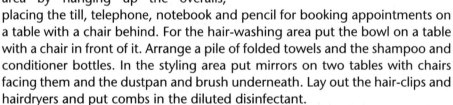

Further ideas

■ Make a display of 'Our hairstyles' (see page 47).
■ Cover a child's eyes with a blindfold and see if he or she can tell who other children are just by feeling their hair.

■ Make a display of 'Our hairstyles' (see page 47).

LEARNING OBJECTIVES
STEPPING STONE
Take initiatives and manage developmentally appropriate tasks.

EARLY LEARNING GOAL
Dress and undress independently and manage their own personal hygiene. (PSED)

GROUP SIZE
Eight children.

HOME LINKS
Suggest that parents and carers encourage their children to comb their own hair and to help by rubbing in the shampoo at bathtime to develop their skills in taking care of themselves.

Sweet singing

What you need
A handkerchief or small scarf.

What to do
Remind the children that Rapunzel had a beautiful singing voice. Tell them that they are going to play a singing game and they will need to learn the following words to sing to the tune of 'The wheels on the bus':

> The Prince heard a voice he didn't know,
> Didn't know, didn't know,
> The Prince heard a voice he didn't know,
> Whose was the voice he heard?

Pick one child to be the Prince then help the other children to sit down in a circle on the floor. Give the handkerchief to the Prince and ask him or her to run round the outside of the circle while everybody sings the song. When you get to the last word of the song, the Prince drops the handkerchief behind the child he or she is passing. This child now stands up and runs round the outside of the circle in the opposite direction to the Prince. The aim is to see who can get back first to sit down in the empty space. The loser becomes the next Prince.

Remind the children that when the Prince heard Rapunzel singing, he didn't know who it was. Can you tell who a person is from his or her singing voice? Some people sing with very deep voices and some with very high voices.

Support and extension
With younger children, invite the child with the handkerchief to hold hands with the Prince and to walk round the circle together, then back to their places. Ask older children to run around the circle twice before they sit down in the empty space.

Further ideas
■ Practise singing the nursery rhyme 'Three Blind Mice', and then see if you can sing as a round. Try to do the same with the song 'London's Burning'.
■ Record the children's voices individually on a tape recorder. Play the tape back to them and see if they can tell which is their own voice.

LEARNING OBJECTIVES
STEPPING STONE
Respond to simple instructions.

EARLY LEARNING GOAL
Sustain attentive listening, responding to what they have heard by relevant comments, questions or actions. (CLL)

GROUP SIZE
12 children.

HOME LINKS
Suggest that parents and carers sing nursery rhymes with their children at home.

Plaits and rope-ladders

LEARNING OBJECTIVES
STEPPING STONE
Show an interest in numbers and counting.

EARLY LEARNING GOAL
Say and use number names in order in familiar contexts. (MD)

GROUP SIZE
Six children.

What you need
The photocopiable sheet 'Tower game' on page 79; two sheets of A4 card; two dice and shakers; six counters in different colours.

Preparation
Make two card copies of the photocopiable sheet as game boards.

What to do
Remind the children that Rapunzel and the Prince planned to escape by using a rope-ladder. Which other ways could they have come down from the tower: using a parachute, fire-engine ladders, a helicopter, a hot-air balloon? Rapunzel's plaits were used like a rope. What kind of people use ropes for climbing? (Mountaineers, tree surgeons.)

Show the children the game boards and ask them to identify the numbers and the pictures of rope-ladders and plaits. Explain that if you land on a rope-ladder, you go down to the square where it ends, and that if you land on a plait you climb up to the square where that starts.

Demonstrate how to play the game by placing a counter on the square marked 'start'. Throw the dice and move the counter the appropriate number of places along the board. For example, if you throw a 4 and land on this rope-ladder it can be ignored because in the game you can only go down a ladder. If you then throw a 1 to move one place into the square marked number 5 you will climb up the plait to square number 7. The aim of the game is to reach number 20 on the board. Continue to give more examples until you are satisfied that the children can play their own games in groups of three.

Support and extension
With younger children only play to number 10 on the board, and let them climb up plaits but do not come down rope-ladders. With older children start at number 20 and subtract the numbers shown on the dice to work down to number 1.

Further ideas
■ When the children know numbers beyond 20, let them play the game on a 'Snakes and Ladders' board.
■ Make a plait using three equal lengths of thick wool tied to a chair-back. Secure the finished plait with an elastic band.

HOME LINKS
Encourage parents and carers to play simple board games with their children to give them practice in taking turns.

Find Rapunzel

What you need
A small doll with long yellow hair; small set of stepladders.

Preparation
If you do not have a suitable doll available you will need to cut lengths of yellow wool into long strands and attach it to the doll's head to look like long golden hair.

What to do
Tell the children to pretend that the doll is Rapunzel. She is going to stand in different places and you want the children to tell you where she is. Place the doll under the stepladder, then up at the top, down at the bottom, in front, behind, next to, between the steps. Each time you position the doll ask the children to tell you where she is. When they are familiar with the positions and their words, ask each child in turn to place the doll where you tell them. For example, 'Put Rapunzel in between the first and second step', 'Put Rapunzel in front of the steps'.

Remind the children that the Prince couldn't find where the sweet singing voice was coming from. He looked everywhere. Where should he have looked to find Rapunzel? He should have looked up to the top of the tower. If you look up what can you see? Lamp-posts, a church steeple, trees, birds or clouds, for example.

Support and extension
With younger children, limit the positions in which you place the doll to the top or bottom of the steps. For older children include more positions for the doll: against, facing, to the left/right, near/far.

Further ideas
■ Ask the children to cover their eyes while you hide the doll somewhere in the room. Give them position word clues of where to find it.
■ Play a game of 'Simon says' with the children. For example, 'Simon says sit on your chair, Simon says put your feet under the chair, Simon says sit next to your chair. Sit on the floor.'
■ Say the action rhyme 'Tall Shop' from *Round and Round the Garden* by Ian Beck and Sarah Williams (Oxford University Press).

LEARNING OBJECTIVES
STEPPING STONE
Observe and use positional language.

EARLY LEARNING GOAL
Use everyday words to describe position. (MD)

GROUP SIZE
Six children.

HOME LINKS
Suggest that parents and carers use positional words when talking to their children.

A tall tower

What you need
A piece of grey plastic pipe 11cm diameter and approximately 40cm tall; sheet of thick grey A3 paper; a dinner plate (28cm diameter); pencil; scissors; stapler; two indelible black marker pens; sticky tape; small piece of yellow card; a long woollen plait (see Further ideas to 'Plaits and rope-ladders' page 50); patchwork fields (see 'Above the world', page 56); four long wooden building blocks; labelling card.

What to do
Explain to the children that a tower is a tall, square or circular building and is usually part of another building. In the past, towers were built tall for defence reasons and to enable them to be used as observation posts. Why was Rapunzel put in the tower? (So nobody could reach her.) Which tower pictures have the children seen? (They may have seen pictures of Blackpool Tower, the Post Office Tower in London, the Eiffel Tower in Paris or the Leaning Tower of Pisa.)

Say that you are going to make a tower together. Share the jobs fairly between the children to ensure that they are all involved in making the tower. Make a cone shape by drawing round a dinner plate onto a sheet of A3 paper, cut round the circle and cut one straight line into the middle, wrap the circle round into cone shape and secure. Draw roof tiles onto the cone with a marker pen and secure it to the pipe tower with sticky tape. Draw builders' brick patterns onto the pipe tower.

Near the top of the tower, stick the yellow card as a small window, mark the window panes and 'hang' the plait from the window. Arrange the patchwork fields across the table top and place the tower in the middle of the fields, stabilising it with the four building blocks. Label the display 'Rapunzel's tower'.

Support and extension
Help younger children with cutting and sticking tasks. Encourage older children to suggest ways of making the various components of the display.

Further ideas
■ Each day alter the length of the plait and the height of the tower (stand it on bricks). Add labels, 'How long is Rapunzel's plait today?' and 'How tall is the tower today?'.
■ Place some toy farm-animals and buildings in the display fields.
■ Build a square tower with the construction toys (don't forget the window).

A knotty problem

What you need
A ball of thick string; scissors; a 50cm measure.

Preparation
Cut the string into at least twenty pieces each 50cm long.

What to do
In the story the Prince took pieces of rope to Rapunzel each time he visited her so that she could make a ladder. Why did she need a rope-ladder? Explain that rope and string are made by twisting together the tough fibres of growing plants such as cotton, hemp and straw. Today, rope is often made from man-made materials such as nylon.

Give the children five pieces of string each and ask them to think of ways that they can use them to make their own rope-ladder. Hopefully, someone will suggest knotting the pieces together. Make sure that the children know how to tie a knot, first using only one piece of string and then tying two end-pieces together. Eventually they may discover that they can link the lengths of string, tying the ends of each link together in a knot, to form a rope chain which could be used for a 'rope-ladder'.

Support and extension
With younger children, use one piece of string only and tie simple knots along its length. For older children link all the individual rope-ladders together; estimate how far their length will reach across the room and then check your estimate.

Further ideas
■ Unravel a piece of string and see how many strands children can count.
■ Turn a skipping rope, and see how many times children can skip before they trip up.
■ Ask what kind of people use ladders in their work. (Window-cleaners, builders, fire-fighters, for example.)
■ Invite children to thread thin string through a large-eyed, blunt needle, then sew some loosely woven fabric to see how important it is to knot the string first.

LEARNING OBJECTIVES
STEPPING STONE
Begin to try out a range of tools and techniques safely.

EARLY LEARNING GOAL
Select the tools and techniques they need to shape, assemble and join materials they are using. (KUW)

GROUP SIZE
Four children.

HOME LINKS
Invite any parents or carers who can recall how to play games with string such as Cat's cradle to come in and demonstrate to the children.

Neighbour's footsteps

What you need
Felt-tipped pen; pencil.

What to do
Hold up the pointed end of the pencil to see if the children know that it is called the 'tip'. Similarly, find out if they know why a felt-tipped pen is so called. Explain that the tip of something is the very end of it and that it is usually pointed.

Ask the children to walk around the room and listen to the noise their feet make. How do you walk when you want to be very quiet? Show the children how to stand on tiptoe and ask them to walk around the room like this. What part of your foot is off the ground when you walk on tiptoe? (Your heel.)

Remind the children that in the story the husband walked on tiptoe in the neighbour's garden. Explain how to play the game 'Neighbour's footsteps'. The children should stand at one end of the room while you face the wall at the other end. Tell them to pretend that they have just climbed into the neighbour's garden, like the husband in the story. They are to creep towards you and the 'lettuce' without you seeing them move. Whenever you look round they have to 'freeze' into statues. If you see them actually moving, they have to go back to the beginning again. The aim is to be able to touch the wall where you are standing without being seen to move.

Support and extension
Tell younger children they don't need to go back to the beginning until the second time you see them moving. When older children reach the neighbour's wall they can take their turn to be the neighbour.

Further ideas
■ Suggest all the different types of people who might walk on tiptoe and why – the parent or carer of a sleeping baby or child, latecomers to the cinema, a ballet dancer, small children who can't reach the light switch, grown-ups walking through puddles!
■ Freeze a balloon full of water than peel off the rubber and float the ice balloon in a bucket of water. You will only be able to see the top of it – like the tip of an iceberg.

Salad faces

What you need
Lettuce (if possible, a curly leafed type); a selection of the following: cherry and large tomatoes, two eggs, a small cucumber or gherkins, carrots, mustard and cress, watercress, beansprouts, spring onions or chives, fresh parsley, coriander and fennel foliage, black olives or currants; small sharp knife; potato peeler; pair of kitchen scissors, grater, colander, chopping board, washing-up bowl; water; paper towels; a dinner plate (or a paper plate) for each child.

Preparation
Hard boil, peel and slice the eggs. Check for any food allergies.

What to do
In the story the wife saw the fresh lettuce growing over the wall and thought it would taste delicious. Which salad vegetables do the children think are delicious? If the salad vegetables were cooked would they still be crispy? Many vegetables can be eaten raw and are very good for you.

Explain that the children are going to use the salad materials to make some funny faces. First ensure the children wash their hands before handling food. Share out the following tasks: wash all the salad ingredients, drain them through the colander and pat dry with the paper towels, halve some of the cherry tomatoes (closely supervise use of the knife), slice the cucumber thinly, grate some of the carrot.

Give the children a plate each and ask them to choose some of the ingredients to make a salad face. Suggest that hair can be made with torn lettuce leaves, parsley, fennel or coriander; eyes can be slices of egg or cucumber with an olive or currant; eyebrows can be grated carrot, cress, bean sprouts or chives; cheeks can be half tomatoes and mouths can be strips of tomato or carrot. When they have finished making their salad faces they can eat them!

Support and extension
Help younger children choose which salad materials to use to represent their face. Encourage older children to be adventurous and creative in their choice of materials.

Further ideas
■ Use more salad vegetables to add extra features to your salad face, such as spring onion bulb earrings, a chive hair bow, a carrot bow-tie, a beansprout moustache or beard.
■ Make a display of different shapes and colours of lettuce.
■ Use toothpicks or cocktail sticks to pin the salad pieces onto a whole potato, carrot, apple or orange to make vegetable creatures.
■ Cut cabbage leaves with scissors, grate some carrot and then mix with mayonnaise or salad cream to make coleslaw.

Above the world

What you need

Deep box; dry sand; eggcup; drinking glass; pencil; cardboard tube; ruler; tin of baby powder; piece of A3 green card; pieces of green and brown fabric; different textured green and brown paper; scissors; PVA glue and spreaders; thick black marker pen.

Preparation

Out of sight of the children pour the sand into the deep box and try to bury the eggcup, glass, pencil, cardboard tube, ruler and baby powder in the sand so that only the top of each object shows.

What to do

Can the children recognise and name the articles that have been buried in the sand? Point out that things look very different when viewed from above.

Explain that if you stand on the ground in a field you can see it all around you. What would you see if you looked at the same field from above? A field in the countryside would have lots of other fields around it. Rapunzel lived in a tall tower and would have been able to look down on a giant patchwork quilt of fields. Tell the children that they are going to make a picture of what Rapunzel might have seen from her window in the tall tower. Cut out irregular pieces of paper and fabric and glue them onto the green card as if they were different fields next to each other. Overlap some field edges so that the card doesn't show through. Finally, draw in some hedge lines with the black marker pen.

Support and extension

With younger children cut out the irregular pieces of paper and fabric ready for them to glue onto the card. Ask older children to make individual patchwork fields for the display 'A tall tower' on page 52.

Further ideas

■ Bury some other articles up to their tops in the sand. Can the children guess what they are?
■ Place a doll's house in the middle of a table and ask the children to sit around it. Can they describe what they can each see? Why do they think that everyone can see different things?

Hansel and Gretel

This is a classic story of how good triumphs over evil as the children manage to outwit their cruel stepmother and the wicked woman and finally return to their loving father. It offers opportunities to create a candy house display and use everyday items to make percussion instruments.

The candy house

What you need
Cardboard box (approximately 24cm × 24cm × 30cm); a piece of cardboard (50cm × 35cm); black paper; craft knife (adult use only); scissors; PVA glue and spreaders; packet of paper hole reinforcers; split-pins; black envelope wrappers from wafer thin mint chocolates; variety of other sweet and chocolate wrappers; large cardboard sweet tube; labelling card and marker pen.

Preparation
Cut the top and bottom flaps off the box to leave only four walls. Cut out squares for windows and a door flap to open and shut. Score and bend the cardboard sheet in half to make a roof and cut out a circle for the chimney.

What to do
Ask the children to help you make a house like the one in the story. Show them how to stick the envelope wrappers onto the roof, overlapping them like tiles (cut more from black paper if necessary). Wedge the large sweet tube in the hole for a chimney. Stick paper hole reinforcers around the windows and doors to look like mints with holes. Cover the rest of the box with sweet wrappers, using a chocolate bar wrapper for the door. Fix the cardboard roof to the box using split-pins and then label the box 'The candy house'.

Ask the children if they were to stay in a candy house like Hansel and Gretel what sorts of problems might there be? If it was hot, the chocolate would melt. Perhaps the birds and animals would try to eat the house. Explain that people in America use the word 'candy' instead of 'sweets'.

Support and extension
Organise younger children to carry out simple tasks such as sticking the paper hole reinforcements on. Invite older children to make suggestions for how to use the available resources to create the candy house.

Further ideas
■ Put some doll's house furniture and play people inside the candy house and let the children pretend that they are Hansel and Gretel.
■ Count how many different types of sweet wrapper have been used.
■ Bake a sponge cake house and decorate it with chocolate-button roof tiles. Cover the walls with sugar-coated chocolate beans and jelly pastilles. Use liquorice type sweets for the door and chimney.

LEARNING OBJECTIVES
STEPPING STONE
Relate and make attachments to members of their group.

EARLY LEARNING GOAL
Work as part of a group or class, taking turns and sharing fairly, understanding that there needs to be agreed values and codes of behaviour for groups of people, including adults and children, to work together harmoniously. (PSED)

GROUP SIZE
Six children.

HOME LINKS
Ask parents and carers to save up sweet wrappers for the children to make the candy house.

Initial blocks

What you need
Pencils; paper; five rectangular pieces of softwood such as balsa (approximately 10cm × 15cm); sandpaper; packet of steel tacks (2cm); five small hammers (not toys); Blu-Tack or Plasticine; thick pencil.

Preparation
Sandpaper the blocks of wood until they are smooth enough for the children to handle. They may be able to do this for themselves.

What to do
Hansel and Gretel's father was a woodcutter who cut down trees for people to use in different ways. What kind of things are made from wood? (Paper, furniture, pencils, bird-tables, sheds, fences.) Woodcutters are sometimes called tree-surgeons because they look after trees to make sure they are safe.

Ask the children to each write their first name on some paper. Make sure that they use a capital letter at the beginning. Explain that this first letter is their initial and that you want them to write it on the block of wood you are going to give them, writing the letter as large as they can to fill the space. Why do people use their initials? Do you think it is because their initials take up less room than their full name?

After each child has written their initial on their block, let them take it in turns to practise hammering tacks into your piece of wood, under close supervision. For extra safety, a blob of Blu-Tack can be used to hold the tack in place. When they have practised sufficiently, let them hammer tacks along the outline of their initial on their own block of wood. There is no need for them to hammer the tacks right in.

Support and extension
With younger children write their initial for them onto the wood, so that they have an outline to follow. Ask older children to use the initials from their first name and second names.

Further ideas
■ Make a list of all the children's initials and see if they can recognise to whom they belong.
■ Initials are used all around us; what does TV mean, and what does 'M' on a traffic sign refer to? (Motorway.) What other initials have the children seen?
■ Try screwing a screw into wood using a screwdriver then compare screws with nails and tacks.

Shapes at night

What you need
Piece of thick A4 card; craft knife (adult use only); mug; sheets of black A4 paper; white or silver crayons for each child; paper-clips.

Preparation
Draw round the base of the mug to make a circle, half-circle and crescent shape on three of the quarters of the thick card. Cut out the shapes with a craft knife to make a moon-phase stencil.

What to do
Explain that the moon does not have its own light. What makes it shine? (The light from the sun.) As the moon moves round the Earth, it is sometimes in a position where there is no sunlight on it and then it can't be seen (the final quarter of paper). This is how the moon was when Hansel and Gretel scattered breadcrumbs – it was hidden and so the night was very dark. When the moon starts to reflect sunlight again it shows up as a very thin crescent called the new moon. Soon half the moon is lit up and then the whole moon is shining. This is called a full moon.

Point to the full moon on the stencil and ask the children what shape it is (a circle), then ask what shape the half moon is (half-circle or semicircle), and finally the new moon (a crescent shape). Secure the stencil over a piece of black paper with some paperclips, and let a child draw the moon outlines with a white or silver crayon. When the outlines have been drawn, pass the stencil to the next child and so on. Once drawn, the outlines can be filled in. Point out that the final quarter of paper has no moon showing at all.

Support and extension
Help younger children by drawing the outlines of the moons for them. Invite older children to write 'new moon', 'half moon' and 'full moon' under the appropriate shapes.

Further ideas
■ Compare a marble to a tennis ball to show the difference in size between the moon and the Earth. Which is bigger? (The Earth.)
■ Sing and dance to 'Sally go round the moon' from *My Very First Mother Goose* by Iona Opie (Walker Books).

LEARNING OBJECTIVES

STEPPING STONE
Show awareness of similarities in shapes in the environment.

EARLY LEARNING GOAL
Talk about, recognise and recreate simple patterns. (MD)

GROUP SIZE
Six children.

HOME LINKS
During winter months ask parents and carers to show their children the different phases of the moon when it can be seen in the night sky.

A pebble trail

What you need
Plenty of small pebbles (from a garden centre or a builder's merchant); colander; bowl of soapy water; paper towels; three containers of smooth white paint; a fine paintbrush for each child; plenty of newspaper; the photocopiable sheet 'Follow the trail' on page 80; coloured card; PVA glue.

Preparation
Wash the pebbles in soapy water, drain them through the colander and rinse them under running water. Leave them to dry thoroughly on the paper towels. Make six copies of the photocopiable sheet using coloured card.

What to do
Remind the children about the trail that Hansel and Gretel left. They did not paint their pebbles, so what made them show up in the dark? (The moonlight.) Explain that if you dig in the ground you will always find rocks and pebbles and these are important in a garden because they help soil drainage and are used as shelter for some creatures.

Lay newspaper over a table then ask the children to take a handful of pebbles each. Let them examine the pebbles before spreading them out on the newspaper in front of them. Ask them to paint as much of each pebble as they can without touching them with their fingers. They will have to leave the paint to dry before turning them all over and painting the other side.

When the pebbles are completely dry, give each child a copy of the photocopiable sheet and invite the children to lay a pebble trail to show Hansel and Gretel the way back home. Use directional and positional language to introduce words such as 'left', 'right', 'along', 'up' and 'down'.

Support and extension
With younger children put the pebbles into a saucer of white paint and let the children stir them round with a fork to cover them in white paint and then lift them out with the fork. Ask older children to stick the pebbles onto the photocopiable sheet with PVA glue to make a permanent trail.

Further ideas
■ Estimate how many pebbles you would be able to carry in one of your pockets and then check to see if your guess was correct.
■ Arrange the pebbles in groups, starting with one and adding one more each time and then count them.
■ Try 'writing' your initials using pebbles – how many do you need?

LEARNING OBJECTIVES
STEPPING STONE
Describe a simple journey.

EARLY LEARNING GOAL
Use everyday words to describe position. (MD)

GROUP SIZE
Six children.

HOME LINKS
Let the children take further copies of the photocopiable sheet home to complete with their parents and carers, using other materials such as small balls of play dough to complete the trail.

Leafy clues

What you need
Six different leaf varieties such as laurel, oak, holly, Scots pine, birch, beech, sycamore, horse chestnut, lilac, ornamental cherry or ivy.

What to do
Remind the children that when Hansel and Gretel were left in the wood they tried to find their way out by remembering the leaves of the trees they had passed, but it was dark and they couldn't see.

Show the children the leaves you have available and let them handle the leaves and compare the sizes and shapes. Point out the leaf edging and show the children how to hold the leaves up to see whether any light shows through. Let them smell the leaves and feel their texture and thickness. Mix all the leaves together and ask the children to sort them into sets. When they have finished ask them to explain how they have sorted them – was it by thickness, shape, size, leaf edge?

What differences did the children notice in the leaves? The shapes vary: some are hand-shaped, some are long and some narrow or spiky. The edges also vary: some are straight, some are jagged like teeth, some are wavy and some have lobed edges like the children's earlobes. Were all the leaves the same thickness? Tell them that thicker leathery leaves such as laurel, holly and ivy are evergreen and do not fall off the trees in autumn like the thinner types of leaves (birch, beech, sycamore).

Support and extension
Let younger children focus on two varieties of leaves only. Ask older children to select the leaves that you ask for: thick, thin, jagged-edged, wavy-edged.

Further ideas
■ Staple different types of leaves to a piece of paper and draw round the edges. Remove the leaves and see the outlines.
■ Collect and sort other things which come from trees such as conkers, acorns, ash-keys and fir cones.
■ Place a thin leaf on a paper towel. Hold it at one end with a finger while tapping the leaf repeatedly with the bristles of a nailbrush. The flesh of the leaf disappears leaving a skeleton of ribs and veins.

LEARNING OBJECTIVES
STEPPING STONE
Examine objects and living things to find out more about them.

EARLY LEARNING GOAL
Investigate objects and materials by using all of their senses as appropriate. (KUW)

GROUP SIZE
Any size

HOME LINKS
Show the children how to make a leaf rubbing, by fastening a thick leaf, vein side up, to a piece of paper with a paper-clip. With paper uppermost, rub a wax crayon lengthways until the impression of the leaf shows. Suggest that they collect some leaves at home and make some more rubbings in the same way.

Bread and butter pudding

What you need
Six medium slices of stale bread; 60g butter; 100g dried apricots (or sultanas); 570ml milk; two eggs; 75g sugar; a 1l glass jug; handwhisk; spoon; spreading knife; chopping board; knife; large baking dish; piece of greaseproof paper.

Preparation
Buy the bread two or three days beforehand so that it will have had time to go stale. Grease the baking dish using a little of the butter and the greaseproof paper. Check for any food allergies and intolerances.

What to do
Ask the children if they can recall why Hansel and Gretel couldn't follow the trail of the breadcrumbs they had dropped. (The birds had eaten them.) What else do birds like to eat? (Worms, insects, seeds, nuts.) Explain that in winter, when the ground is frozen, it is important to feed the birds with tiny pieces of your own food, such as bacon rind and fat, or bits of cheese and apple.

Explain that you are going to use some bread to make a pudding. Show the children how to pull the crusts off the slices of bread and put them to one side. With the middles of the slices, ask them to make breadcrumbs by rubbing the bread between their fingers.

Cut the apricots into small pieces and add them to the crumbs. Break the eggs into the jug and whisk them with the sugar, gradually adding the milk. Pour this mixture over the breadcrumbs in the baking dish; stir and leave to stand for half an hour so the breadcrumbs absorb the milk and swell.

Tear the crusts into chunks, place them on top of the pudding and push them down gently. Dot the butter over the surface and bake in the oven at 180°C (350°F, Gas Mark 4) for about an hour, until the custard is set and the crusts have gone brown and crispy. Sit down and enjoy a portion of pudding each!

Support and extension
Invite the younger children to help tear up the bread and to make breadcrumbs. Ask older children to cut up the apricots, whisk the eggs and help to pour the custard mixture over the breadcrumbs.

Further ideas
■ Place a bird-table near your window and put some wild bird seed on it. Draw the different kinds of birds that visit the table.
■ Tie some string on a pine cone then dip it in some melted fat before rolling it in biscuit crumbs, peanuts, currants and breakfast cereals. Hang this bird cone outside and watch the birds peck at it.

Which way out?

What you need
12 pieces of A4 cardboard; thick black marker pen; twelve chairs.

Preparation
Bend the pieces of card in half to make roof-top-shaped signs and draw one large bold arrow on each card – three cards with arrows pointing north, three east, three west and three south.

What to do
Ask where the children have seen arrows before for example, in car parks, at hospitals, on road signs. If there had been arrows on the trees in the forest, Hansel and Gretel would have been able to find their way home easily.

Say that you are going to make a trail and the children will have to follow the arrows to get around it. Show the children the arrow cards and ensure that they know what they are and they show you which way to go. Let them have several practice turns in facing the direction that you show them on the arrows. Explain that the north arrow means go straight ahead. Ask them to help you dot the chairs around the room and place the prepared arrow cards on them so that they are pointing in different directions. The children can now take it in turns to walk around the room following the direction of the arrows.

Support and extension
Walk the route with the younger children to get them used to the idea of following the direction of arrows. With older children, keep changing the directions of the arrows on the route to make it more challenging.

Further ideas
■ Ask the children to find the North and South Poles on a globe.
■ With the children, use the midday sun to decide which direction is south. Hold a magnetic compass in your hand and show how the needle always swings round to point north regardless of the way you are facing. The other end of the needle always points south.
■ Teach the children the compass points and ask them to draw arrows pointing north, south, east and west.
■ Explain that compasses contain magnets. Hand round some magnets and paperclips and allow the children to experiment.

Sounds like a story

LEARNING OBJECTIVES
STEPPING STONE
Explore and learn how sounds can be changed.

EARLY LEARNING GOAL
Recognise and explore how sounds can be changed, sing simple songs from memory, recognise repeated sounds and sound patterns and match movements to music. (CD)

GROUP SIZE
12 children.

What you need
Piece of sandpaper; pair of shoes; paper bag full of milk-bottle tops (pieces of foil); pebbles; tea-towel; plastic bottle half full of pebbles; two telephone directories; a bunch of keys; greaseproof paper; silver foil; empty washing-up bottle; nailbrush; newspaper; bag of small construction bricks.

What to do
If the children have ever been for a walk in the woods like Hansel and Gretel, what sounds did they hear? In bed at night, when most people are asleep, you can hear all sorts of sounds which you don't hear in the day. What are they? (Sounds made by central heating, creaking stairs, owls hooting, cats.)

Show the children the different sounds that can be made by using different objects (see below), then hand out the objects. While you read the children the story of Hansel and Gretel suggest that they make sounds at particular moments in the story:

When the woodcutter is mentioned.
(Rub the sandpaper together in a sawing rhythm.)
When the parents' plans are overheard. *(Make whispering noises.)*
When Hansel and Gretel creep out to collect pebbles.
('Walk' the shoes very quietly on the floor.)
When they walk through the forest. *(Shake the bottle-tops bag.)*
When Hansel secretly drops pebbles. *(Drop pebbles onto a tea-towel.)*
When the parents leave Hansel and Gretel.
(Shake the bottle of pebbles for heavy feet crunching.)
When the stepmother is furious.
(Bang your hands on the telephone directories.)
When the bedroom door is locked and when Hansel is locked up.
(Jangle a bunch of keys.)
When the father makes them a fire.
(Shake the greaseproof paper and silver foil for crackling and burning sounds.)
When the night sounds in the forest start.
(Hoot like an owl, squeeze the washing-up bottle for a mouse.)
When the wind blows. *(Brush the newspaper.)*
When Hansel and Gretel grab the jewellery.
(Shake the bag of construction bricks.)
When the oven door opens and slams. *(Open and close the door.)*
When Hansel and Gretel run back to their father. *(Beat hands on chest.)*

Support and extension
With younger children call them by name each time you want them to make 'their' sound. Encourage older children to make their sounds whenever they think it is appropriate in the story.

Further ideas
■ Can children identify sounds with their eyes shut?
■ Invite children to blow recorders to make animal sounds.

HOME LINKS
Encourage the children to hunt around at home for suitable items to make sound effects and to practise making different sounds with them.

Beads and bracelets

What you need
Small block of wood; piece of sandpaper; five mugs of fine sawdust (can be bought medicated in bags from a petshop); one mug of dry wallpaper paste (no fungicide); four cups of water; large mixing bowl; fork; six thin knitting needles or skewers; name labels; pencils; six short shoelaces; aprons.

What to do
Hansel and Gretel's father made sawdust by the sawing action of cutting trees down. What else can sawdust be used for? (Bedding for pet hamsters, or in making chipboard, for example.) In the past it was used to stop people slipping on floors (in a butcher's shop) and also for stuffing dolls.

Show the children what happens when you sandpaper the wooden block. (It makes sawdust.) Mix the mugs of sawdust and wallpaper paste and then add the water. Ask the children to help knead it into a workable dough, adding more water if necessary.

Explain that you are going to use this dough to make some jewellery. Ask: What is jewellery made from? Often it is made from gold or silver and contains precious stones.

Show the children how to make beads (1.5cm diameter) by rolling the dough between the flattened palms of both hands. Push each bead onto a knitting needle. Label each needle and leave the beads to dry naturally (for three or four days). Thread the beads onto a shoelace and tie into bracelets.

Support and extension
Give younger children a measured amount of dough to make each bead. Help older children to make very small beads, thread them onto very thin needles and secure with thread.

Further ideas
■ Paint the beads and glaze them with PVA glue before threading.
■ Add pieces of cut drinking straws and short pieces of macaroni to the sawdust beads. Arrange them into different patterns before threading to make a necklace.
■ Flatten the sawdust dough and use pastry cutters to make different shapes. Push a hole through the shapes and when they are dry they can be threaded into pendants.
■ Use sawdust dough to create a forest display (see 'In the forest', page 66).

LEARNING OBJECTIVES
STEPPING STONE
Understand that different media can be combined.

EARLY LEARNING GOAL
Explore colour, texture, shape, form and space in two or three dimensions. (CD)

GROUP SIZE
Six children.

HOME LINKS
Send home the recipe for sawdust dough for children to make a batch with their parents and carers.

In the forest

What you need
Dark blue lining paper; large piece of matching paper; green activity paper; corrugated and plain card; five pots of ready-mixed paints: yellow, orange, red, brown, black; saucers for paint; circle template; silver paint; PVA adhesive and spreaders; Blu-Tack; marker pen; pencil; scissors; stapler; fresh sawdust; wallpaper paste; water; real leaves such as laurel, ivy, horse chestnut and lilac.

Preparation
Make sawdust dough (see 'Beads and bracelets', page 65) and shape long thin 'sausages'. Flatten these into tree-trunk shapes leaving two of them short and stubby for stumps. Let the dough dry. Line the wall display area with dark blue paper.

What to do
On the piece of blue paper, randomly fingerpaint a fire with different colours. Make leaf shapes on the green paper (see Further ideas in 'Leafy clues', page

There is a full moon in the forest tonight

61) and cut them out. Draw shapes for a new moon, half moon and full moon on the card, paint them silver and cut them out. Staple the fire to the middle of the display and arrange tree trunks around it. Add some strips of corrugated card for branches and pin a real leaf to the top of each tree.

Ask the children to sort and match the paper leaves to each tree before sticking them onto the branches. Explain that although growing trees is very important, we sometimes need to cut them down to give other trees more room to grow or to provide wood to make things. Stick some fresh sawdust at the base of the tree stumps. Write a caption 'There is a ___ moon in the forest tonight.' Write additional labels, 'new', 'half' and 'full'. Blu-Tack one of the moon shapes into position and ask the children to choose the correct label for the caption.

Support and extension
Ask younger children to fingerpaint the fire in place. Encourage older children to sort and match the leaves before sticking them in place.

Further ideas
■ Draw Hansel and Gretel, some woodland creatures and silver stars to add to the display.
■ Collect some fallen leaves to add to the forest floor of the display.
■ Create displays for other favourite stories that the children suggest.

Jack and the Beanstalk

Jack and his widowed mother are very poor. They live in a tiny cottage, and when their cow cannot give milk anymore, Jack's mother tells him to sell the cow at the market so they have some money to buy food.

On the way to market, Jack meets a man who offers to give him five magic beans for the cow. Jack is happy to do this and runs back home with the beans. His mother is very cross with Jack because they need money, not beans! She is so angry that she throws the beans out of the window and sends Jack to bed without having his tea.

Next morning, Jack and his mother are amazed to see that the beans have grown into the most enormous beanstalk. It has a stem as thick as a tree, stretching high into the clouds above their heads. Jack begins to climb the huge beanstalk, fighting his way between the huge leaves. Right at the top, he finds a winding road leading up to a gleaming castle, towering above him. He arrives at the castle and in the gigantic kitchen, he meets a giant woman.

Jack is very hungry and he asks her for some food. She kindly gives him an enormous bowl of porridge, but before he can eat anything the ground shakes and a thunderous voice echoes around. The woman tells Jack to hide before her husband the giant arrives crying, 'Fee-fi-fo-fum, I smell the blood of an Englishman, Be he alive, or be he dead, I'll grind his bones to make my bread!'.

The giant doesn't find anyone and so he eats his dinner. His magic harp sings soothing music while his magic hen lays golden eggs. After eating his dinner he falls asleep. Jack grabs the magic hen and runs away, but the harp makes a noise and the giant chases after Jack.

Jack quickly climbs down the beanstalk, and when he gets to the bottom, he uses his axe to hack down the beanstalk. The giant is following Jack down the beanstalk. He falls to his death when Jack cuts the beanstalk down.

So Jack and his mother have the hen which lays the golden eggs and all the money they need, and they live together happily ever after – thanks to the five magic beans!

Pauline Kenyon

Snow White

When Snow White was born, her mother, the young queen died. The king remarried, and his new wife was the most beautiful, but the most vain woman in all his kingdom. Every day she would stand in front of her magic mirror and ask, 'Mirror, mirror on the wall, who is the fairest one of all?' and the mirror would reply, 'Queen, you are the fairest one of all!'. Time passed and Snow White grew into a lovely young woman. When the proud queen asked the mirror her usual question, she was horrified to hear, 'Queen, you were the fairest, it is true. But now, Snow White is more beautiful than you!'.

The queen was very jealous of Snow White and she plotted to kill her. She ordered her huntsman to take Snow White into the woods and kill her, bringing back her heart. The huntsman knew that murder was wrong, so he took Snow White into the deepest woods and left her there, taking back the heart of a deer.

Snow White wandered into the forest until she found a tiny cottage and went inside. Upstairs she found seven little beds and she was so tired that she lay down to sleep. Later, seven dwarfs returned home from their work mining gold in the mountains and discovered Snow White! They agreed that she could stay with them and they warned her to take care and not let any visitors into the cottage. For they knew that the evil queen would find out that Snow White was alive and would come looking for her. The dwarfs were right. One day the queen dressed as an old woman pedlar, came to the cottage and sold Snow White a magic comb which poisoned her head. The dwarfs found her unconscious, but they managed to save her.

The queen tried again. She came to the cottage disguised as a farmer's wife and gave Snow White a poisoned apple. This time, the dwarfs were too late to save her life.

Snow White was put into a glass coffin. A prince found the coffin and entranced by her beauty, he lifted the lid, the apple fell from her lips and she woke up. The couple fell in love and were married. When the evil queen heard the news she was so angry that she fell down dead and Snow White lived happily ever after.

Pauline Kenyon

The Little Red Hen

One morning the Little Red Hen found some wheat seed among her feed. 'Perfect for bread,' she said, 'Now who will help me plant these seeds?'. She looked around hopefully at the other farmyard animals.

'Not I!' purred Cat, curling back to sleep.

'Not I!' barked Dog, snoozing in the sun.

'Not I!' grunted Pig, rolling over in the mud.

'Oh well,' sighed Hen, 'come on Chicks, let's do it ourselves'.

So Hen tended and cared for those seeds. She hoed, weeded and watered them until the wheat was tall and strong, ready for harvesting.

'Who will help me harvest the wheat?' asked Hen hopefully.

'Not me!' yawned Cat, stretching out her claws.

'Not me!' barked Dog, chewing his bone.

'Not me!' grunted Pig, flipping her ears.

'Oh well,' sighed Hen, 'let's do it ourselves Chicks'. So they did.

'Well now,' said Hen, 'who will help me take these sacks for milling?'

'Not I!' meowed Cat, turning the other way.

'Not I!' growled Dog, burying his bone.

'Not I!' grunted Pig, wallowing in her puddle.

So Little Red Hen heaved the heavy sacks onto a cart and tugged them down the mill. She was tired when she got back, but looked at her hungry chicks and said, 'Well now, who will help me make my bread?'

'Not me!' hissed Cat, sneaking out of the kitchen.

'Not me!' barked Dog, sloping off for a snooze.

'Not me!' grunted Pig, waddling back to her sty. 'Oh well,' sighed Hen, putting on her apron. So Hen mixed and kneaded, she smoothed and shaped until four lovely loaves could be left to rise. She popped the bread in the oven and a delicious smell filled the room.

'Well now,' said Hen 'who will help to eat my bread?' All the other animals rushed up.

'I will!' purred Cat, eyes as big as saucers.

'I will!' dribbled Dog, wagging his tail.

'I will!' grunted Pig, snorting and nosing.

'Oh no!' snapped Hen, with a shiver of feathers. 'You lazy lumps left the work up to me. So keep watching. Here Chicks, fresh bread for tea!'

Lesley Clark

Goldilocks and The Three Bears

There was once a family of bears who loved to eat porridge for breakfast. One morning the porridge smelled delicious but it was much too hot. 'I know,' said Daddy, 'let's go for a walk in the woods while it cools down'. So Mummy bear, Daddy bear and Baby bear set off.

Minutes later, a little girl called Goldilocks passed by their cottage. She smelled the porridge, and as she was very hungry, she peeped inside. Nobody at home! When she saw the three bowls of porridge she just had to try some. She dipped her finger in the biggest bowl, 'Too salty!' she cried. She tasted the next bowl, 'Horribly sweet!' But when she tasted the little bowl, it was perfect, so she ate it all up.

Next, Goldilocks went to sit on a large old chair. 'Too hard!' she said. She tried a medium-sized chair but sunk down to the springs, 'Too soft!' she said. Then she spied a small wooden stool, which looked just right... until CRACK! She broke it to bits. Goldilocks trotted upstairs to find somewhere to rest. She saw three beds and flung herself on the largest. 'Oh!' she screamed. 'Hard as nails!' So she tried the medium-sized bed, but that was soft as butter. Last of all, she snuggled into the smallest bed and fell fast asleep.

Meanwhile, the three hungry bears returned to find the cottage door wide open. 'Who's been eating my porridge?' roared Daddy bear. 'Who's been eating my porridge?' asked Mummy bear. 'Who's been eating my porridge so it's all gone?' cried Baby bear, holding up his empty bowl. Just then, Daddy noticed a lump in his chair. 'Who's been sitting in my chair?' he bellowed. 'Who's been sitting in my chair?' echoed Mummy bear, and 'Who's been sitting on my stool and broken it to bits?' wailed Baby bear.

The bears dashed upstairs and Daddy bear yelled, 'Who's been sleeping in my bed?'. 'Who's been sleeping in my bed?' asked Mummy bear. But they both rushed over as Baby bear gave a shriek, 'Oooh! Who's been sleeping in my bed? And LOOK, she's still there!'. The bears crowded around Goldilocks, giving her such a fright! She dashed past the bears out through the doors and disappeared into the woods. Of course, the bears never saw her again. As for them, they made some more porridge, mended the stool and felt much better!

Lesley Clark

Rapunzel

A man and his wife were very excited to be having a baby. One day the wife was feeling tired and fancied eating some lettuce. Her husband crept into the neighbour's garden on tiptoe, and had gathered a basketful of the lettuce when suddenly the neighbour appeared. She was very angry and would only let him take the lettuce if he promised to give her the new baby. He was so frightened that he agreed.

No sooner was their daughter born than the neighbour, an old woman, came to take her away. The old woman called the baby Rapunzel and looked after her well. When she grew up she was so beautiful that the witch wanted to keep her for herself. She locked her in a room at the top of a tall tower, which had no doors or staircase and only one small window.

Whenever the old woman visited, she would call, 'Rapunzel, Rapunzel, let down your hair,' and then would climb up the girl's plaits. Rapunzel was very lonely and spent her time singing, drawing and plaiting her hair. One day a Prince passed by and heard the most beautiful singing. He looked everywhere to discover who was singing and was about to leave when a paper dart landed at his feet. The message on it said 'Hide in the woods till nightfall'.

The Prince hid and watched as the old woman climbed up Rapunzel's hair. When she had gone, he too called, 'Rapunzel, Rapunzel, let down your hair,' and climbed up to meet Rapunzel. They fell in love, and made plans for her escape.

Everytime the Prince visited he took a piece of string for Rapunzel to make into a rope-ladder. One day the old woman saw the rope-ladder and found out about the Prince. She was so angry that she cut off Rapunzel's plaits and took her to a place far away. Next time the Prince came, it was the old woman, not Rapunzel, who let down the hair. He was so frightened that he fell from the plaits onto some sharp rose thorns which pierced his eyes and made him blind.

He wandered blindly through the forest for many years until one day he heard some sweet singing. Rapunzel cried tears of joy to find her Prince again, and when two of her tears splashed onto his eyes he was able to see again. He took her back to his castle, married her and they lived happily ever after.

Jenny Morris

Hansel and Gretel

A poor woodcutter lived with his family at the edge of a forest. They were often short of food, and one evening the children, Hansel and Gretel, overheard their stepmother persuading their father to get rid of them by abandoning them in the forest. Hansel and Gretel were very upset, but they thought of a plan and crept out to collect some pebbles from the garden.

The next day, as the family walked into the forest, Hansel secretly dropped the pebbles from his pocket, one at a time. Soon their stepmother said, 'You children rest here while your father and I go to cut some wood. We'll be back soon.' But by nightfall, they still hadn't returned. Fortunately, the children could follow the trail of their dropped pebbles which shone in the full moon. When they arrived home, their father was overjoyed, but their stepmother was not. Soon, they heard their stepmother planning to get rid of them again. They wanted to collect more pebbles, but she had locked their bedroom door.

Next morning, their stepmother gave Hansel and Gretel a piece of bread each. Secretly they dropped crumbs of bread along the way to the forest. When they reached the middle of the forest, their father made them a fire before he and their stepmother left. They did not return, so the children looked for the breadcrumbs to follow. But the birds hadn't left a single crumb! Hansel and Gretel were very frightened and tried to remember which trees they had passed by looking at the leaves, but there was not enough light from the new moon to see. They wandered round and round in the forest, completely lost until they stumbled upon a candy house made of sweets, biscuits and chocolates. They were so hungry that they helped themselves to pieces of house!

A woman came out of the candy house and invited them in for drinks. But she was not a good woman. She locked Hansel up for a week, feeding him tasty snacks to fatten him. Then she told Gretel to light the oven. When the woman opened the oven door to test the heat, Gretel pushed her into the oven and slammed the door. Gretel rushed to free Hansel. They grabbed some jewellery and ran through the forest, right into the arms of their father, who was trying to find them. When they reached home, they found that their stepmother had left, and the three of them lived very happily without her!

Jenny Morris

Tell the story

Make a dwarf

Find our clothes

Farmyard animals

Then and now

SCHOLASTIC **77**

Size it up!

Tower game

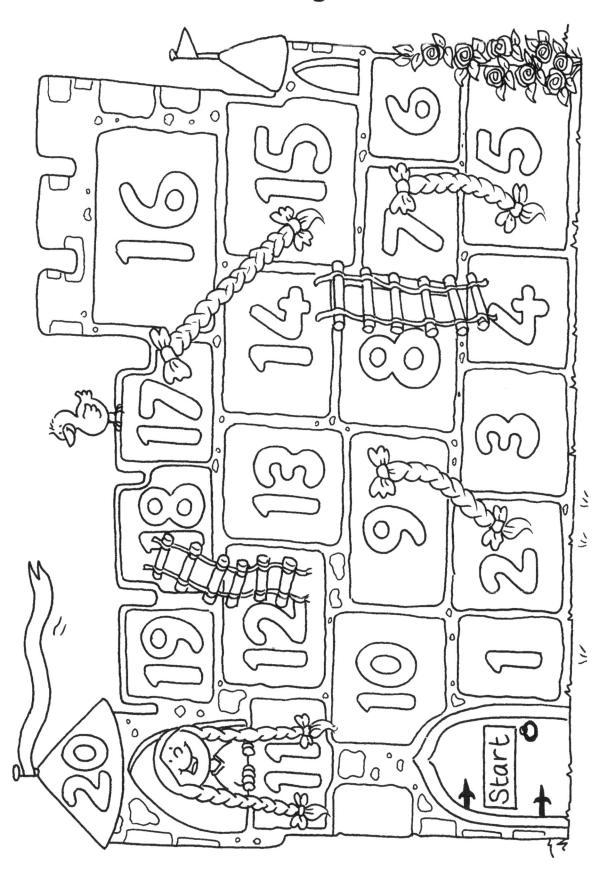

Follow the trail

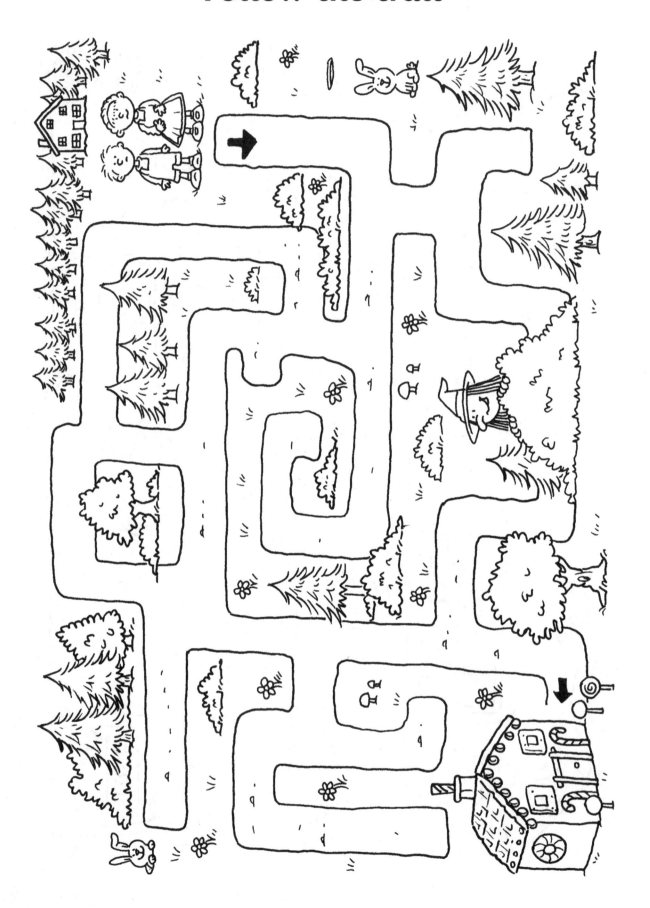